Then, out of the cor

emerge from the bank manager's office with her gun up
and pointed at the back of the last robber's head. "Drop
that pistol and let the woman go or I'll blow your brains
all over the wall!"

The man slowly lowered and then dropped his pistol.
The hostage he held pinned in the crook of his arm
fainted dead away. Longarm relaxed and said with relief, "Why, Miss Sierra Sue, I'm sure grateful for your
help."

"My pleasure," she replied, coming over to stand
beside him. "Don't give it a second thought, Marshal
Long."

Custis started forward to retrieve the bank robber's
fallen gun, and that's when Sierra Sue used the barrel of
her pearl-handled revolver to split the back of his head
wide open. He pitched forward and was instantly unconscious.

"Sorry about that," she said to Longarm with a sad
shake of her head. "But I expect you'll mend in time.
It was either crack your skull or put a bullet in your
brisket."

→→ TABOR EVANS ←←

LONGARM

AND
SIERRA SUE

JOVE BOOKS, NEW YORK

THE BERKLEY PUBLISHING GROUP
Published by the Penguin Group
Penguin Group (USA) Inc.
375 Hudson Street, New York, New York 10014, USA
Penguin Group (Canada), 90 Eglinton Avenue East, Suite 700, Toronto, Ontario M4P 2Y3, Canada
(a division of Pearson Penguin Canada Inc.)
Penguin Books Ltd., 80 Strand, London WC2R 0RL, England
Penguin Group Ireland, 25 St. Stephen's Green, Dublin 2, Ireland (a division of Penguin Books Ltd.)
Penguin Group (Australia), 250 Camberwell Road, Camberwell, Victoria 3124, Australia
(a division of Pearson Australia Group Pty. Ltd.)
Penguin Books India Pvt. Ltd., 11 Community Centre, Panchsheel Park, New Delhi—110 017, India
Penguin Group (NZ), 67 Apollo Drive, Rosedale, North Shore 0632, New Zealand
(a division of Pearson New Zealand Ltd.)
Penguin Books (South Africa) (Pty.) Ltd., 24 Sturdee Avenue, Rosebank, Johannesburg 2196,
South Africa

Penguin Books Ltd., Registered Offices: 80 Strand, London WC2R 0RL, England

This is a work of fiction. Names, characters, places, and incidents either are the product of the author's
imagination or are used fictitiously, and any resemblance to actual persons, living or dead, business
establishments, events, or locales is entirely coincidental.

LONGARM AND SIERRA SUE

A Jove Book / published by arrangement with the author

PRINTING HISTORY
Jove edition / October 2009

Copyright © 2009 by Penguin Group (USA) Inc.
Cover illustration by Miro Sinovcic.

ISBN: 978-0-515-14702-5

JOVE®
Jove Books are published by The Berkley Publishing Group,
a division of Penguin Group (USA) Inc.,
375 Hudson Street, New York, New York 10014.
JOVE® is a registered trademark of Penguin Group (USA) Inc.
The "J" design is a trademark of Penguin Group (USA) Inc.

PRINTED IN THE UNITED STATES OF AMERICA

10 9 8 7 6 5 4 3 2 1

Chapter 1

It was a breezy and cool spring morning in May when
Deputy United States Marshal Custis Long first saw
the woman he would soon come to know as Sierra Sue.
She was riding a palomino mare right down the center
of busy Colfax Avenue, and her long black hair shone
like the sun striking a raven's outstretched wing. The
young woman was so strikingly beautiful that men
froze on the sidewalks and stared with unconcealed
admiration. Sierra Sue was tall and buxom, with long,
shapely legs wrapped in fringed and tight-fitting buckskin chaps, matching a beaded leather shirt that made
no attempt to conceal the perfection of her large, jig-
gling breasts. She wore a pearl-handled revolver on her
hip, and there was a well-oiled Winchester repeater in
her saddle scabbard, both telling everyone that this was
a woman who was prepared to defend herself and her
belongings.

If Sierra Sue was aware of all the attention she was
receiving that busy Denver morning, she didn't show it.
Instead, her dark eyes were fixed straight ahead and

under a Stetson, her lovely face was a study of concentration as she came upon the huge sandstone Bank of Denver. Reining up her palomino mare, she dismounted in a smooth, graceful motion, and then tied her horse to a lamppost and unfastened a pair of bulging and obviously heavy saddlebags. She easily slung the saddlebags over her shoulder, and moved toward the bank, passing by Custis Long.

Always the gentleman, Longarm tipped his snuff brown and flat-brimmed hat to the gorgeous woman and reached to open the heavy oak door of the bank. "Mornin', miss."

At the sound of his deep voice, Sierra Sue's head turned and she studied him for just an instant, then said, "You're wearing a gun and a badge. Are you this city's marshal?"

"No," he replied, trying to keep from focusing on her chest. "I'm a United States marshal. My name is Custis Long and I am at your service."

"I'm known as Sierra Sue," she said, giving him a frank and approving appraisal. "Most people call me plain old Sue."

"There is nothing plain about you, if I may be so bold to state the truth."

She laughed. "May I ask you a question?"

He nodded. "Anything."

"Is this an *honest* and prosperous bank, Marshal?"

The question caught him by surprise, but he quickly recovered to say, "This bank is as honest as the day is long and I trust it with my own small savings. It's been here since the beginning and has played a big role in making Denver the fine city that it is today. And as for being prosperous, I'd say that it has no equal in the West."

"That's exactly what I wanted to hear," she said, giving him a dazzling smile. "That's why I've come so far to make a deposit."

"You're making a wise choice," he heard himself say.

Sierra Sue looked down at the Colt on his hip. "Are you pretty good with that pistol?"

"Fair to middlin'."

"I'll bet you're being modest. And do I detect a Southern drawl?"

"I was born and raised in West Virginia."

"I've never been there, but I do admire a gentleman of the South and a man who can handle himself in a fight."

"I'm not a braggart," he said with modesty. "You look like you might be able to handle that pearl-handled revolver strapped on your hip."

"Like you, I'm fair to middlin' with a gun," she told him, taking his full measure with her eyes and seeming to like what she saw. "I wish you a good and healthy day."

Sierra Sue was so beautiful he couldn't stop grinning, and when she entered the bank, he just naturally followed her like a pet puppy. Once inside the impressive bank with its great murals, waxed marble floors, towering ceiling, and dark carved wooden frescoes, Longarm remembered that he did have a deposit to make into his own account, and happily stepped in the line behind the young woman and whispered, "I've never seen you before in Denver."

"That's probably because I've never been here before. I've come all the way from the Sierra Nevada Mountains." Without turning her head from the row of tellers' cages, she asked, "Have you ever been to Lake Tahoe, Marshal?"

Seeing an opportunity for conversation, Longarm brightened as if he and Sue had been raised in the same small town and thus had a world of things in common to talk about. "As a matter of fact, I have. Lake Tahoe is the prettiest lake I've ever seen, but I remember that its sky blue water is as clear and cold as ice even in the heat of midsummer."

"Yes, it is," she agreed just as the next available teller eagerly motioned her forward to his cage.

Longarm watched as the stunning young woman said a few hushed words to the teller, and then removed a gold nugget from one of the saddlebags and placed it in the teller's hand. The teller's eyes widened, and hushed words were exchanged. He excused himself, and then hurried off to the bank manager's office. A few moments later, the manager appeared and gave a profuse greeting to the woman, and then ushered her inside his office before closing the door for privacy.

"Next?" another teller called, motioning to Longarm to step forward.

Longarm went ahead and made his small deposit, but his mind was not really on banking. Were Sierra Sue's saddlebags packed with gold nuggets? If so, she had been boldly transporting a fortune in gold. Who was this woman and why had she come all the way from California to deposit such a fortune here in Denver?

Being a very curious man, and also an admirer of

feminine beauty, Longarm was intrigued and determined to find the answers to these questions. He also wanted to meet this unusual woman again, and perhaps even advance their brief acquaintance, so he went outside and lit a cheroot, then waited for Sierra Sue to reappear. It was still early in the day and he knew that his absence at the U.S. marshal's office would not be noted.

Longarm was so absorbed in his deliberations about Sierra Sue that he hardly noticed three horsemen who dismounted just half a block up Colfax and checked their sidearms before advancing up the sidewalk. They were large men who walked shoulder to shoulder, causing other pedestrians to step aside or be trampled. One of the men glanced at Longarm as he grabbed the bank's door and threw it open. Longarm figured the trio to be cowboys who were just making a deposit like himself.

"Mornin'," the third one said with a smile as he nodded in greeting. He was young and quite handsome; his eyes dropped to rest on Longarm's badge. With a smile, he said, "Fine mornin', ain't it, Marshal?"

"Fine indeed," Longarm answered.

"I saw a man lying in the street with a bloodied head the next block over," the man said. "He looked to be hurt pretty bad and there were some drunks picking his pockets."

"Is that a fact?"

"It is," the man said. "I just figured you'd like to know so you could help the poor fella."

"Appreciate the information." Longarm didn't move.

"No trouble," the man said, going on into the bank and closing the door behind him.

Longarm considered going to the fallen man's aid,

but he was a United States marshal, not a local lawman. And besides, something about the three strangers just struck him in the wrong way. He decided to stay put for a few more minutes and then go to the fallen man's aid.

Maybe three minutes passed while Longarm smoked and wondered why he was feeling an alarm going off inside his head, a faint warning that something was seriously amiss. And just when he decided that he really had better go and investigate what was going on with the fallen and injured man, from inside the bank he heard a scream.

Longarm's cheroot fell from his lips and his big hand reached for his Colt revolver. "They're trying to hold the bank up!" Longarm said, amazed at their audacity.

Longarm's first instinct was to burst inside with his gun blazing, but he quickly pushed back that notion. Instead, he eased the bank's heavy door open just a crack so that he could look inside and find out exactly what was happening. Hard past experience had taught him that the very last thing he wanted to do was to get into a wild shoot-out, because that would certainly get a lot of innocent bank customers and employees wounded and even killed. No, much better to check out what was happening, he decided, and then to wait just outside this door and get the drop on the thieves after they exited the bank. The trio would be running for their horses, and then Longarm could come up from behind and either arrest or, as a last resort, kill them.

That was his plan and it seemed sensible, as Longarm checked his own pistol, wishing that he had another law officer at his side or that he was holding a shotgun to bring into deadly play.

"Don't kill us!" someone inside shrieked.

The plea told Longarm that he could not afford to wait outside any longer. With his gun up and cocked, he threw open the heavy bank door and jumped inside, eyes swinging from one side of the lobby to the other, rapidly trying to identify the bank robbers.

"Freeze!" he shouted. "United States marshal! Drop those guns!"

The three men had no intention of dropping their guns. Instead, they whirled and started to fire. Longarm's first bullet caught a thief squarely in the throat. He choked and his gun fell to the floor a moment before he followed. A bullet whip-cracked past Longarm's face, and he opened up on the other two men in an exchange of smoke and gunfire. Longarm felt a bullet crease his cheekbone, and another bullet strike his holster and knock him off balance. He pulled his trigger as fast as he could, and three fountains of blood began spurting from another robber's chest a moment before he toppled over dead.

But the last gunman, the handsome fellow who had spoken to Longarm outside the bank just moments earlier, had suddenly grabbed a hostage as a shield, his muscular arm tight around her neck. "Drop that Colt, Marshal! Drop it or I'll kill this lady!" he warned, putting the muzzle of his gun against her head.

The woman was in her fifties and all the blood had left her face. She began to sob hysterically.

"You aren't getting out of here alive," Longarm promised, his gun still up and aimed at the last bank robber. "You had better surrender."

"I'm calling this play, Marshal. What's it to be?"

Longarm felt certain he could kill the gunman, but it would take a perfect shot and the hostage was squirming and fighting for her life. If she moved just an inch or two in the wrong direction, Longarm was afraid that his bullet might find the wrong target.

Then, out of the corner of his eye, he saw Sierra Sue emerge from the bank manager's office with her gun up and pointed at the back of the last robber's head. "Drop that pistol and let the woman go or I'll blow your brains all over the wall!"

The man slowly lowered and then dropped his pistol. The hostage he held pinned in the crook of his arm fainted dead away. Longarm relaxed and said with relief, "Why, Miss Sierra Sue, I'm sure grateful for your help."

"My pleasure," she replied, coming over to stand beside him. "Don't give it a second thought, Marshal Long."

Custis started forward to retrieve the bank robber's fallen gun, and that's when Sierra Sue used the barrel of her pearl-handled revolver to split the back of his head wide open. He pitched forward and was instantly unconscious.

"Sorry about that," she said to Longarm with a sad shake of her head. "But I expect you'll mend in time. It was either crack your skull or put a bullet in your brisket."

The handsome bank robber snatched up his fallen gun and spun around toward the shocked bank customers and tellers. "If anyone so much as moves or makes a peep, I'll kill them."

Another customer fainted, this time a frail-looking merchant named Olaf Peterson.

"Did you get what we came all this way for, Sue?"

"I was just about to," she replied. "Keep everyone under control because this will only take a minute or two."

"Then put a move on so we can scat!"

Sierra Sue stepped over the unconscious Longarm and hurried back into the bank manager's office. She had noted that the plaque on this man's desk read, CHARLES BODNEY II, BANK PRESIDENT. "Where is your damned thieving father? Charles Bodney the First?"

"He's dead," the young man stammered. "We buried my father two weeks ago. Who . . . who are you?"

"Your father cheated my father out of a California gold mine many years ago. He shot and killed my dad, and then he took full title to their rich mining claim on the American River."

"That can't be true!"

"It is true. Your father sold the river claim for a fortune just three days after my father's funeral, and left California on the run. It's taken my brother and me years to find out that Charles Bodney the First came here to Denver and founded this bank."

"I don't believe you!" The young bank owner and president threw up his hands. "My father was a pillar of this entire community. One of the most respected men in Colorado, and he played a huge role in building and developing this city!"

"It doesn't matter what he did after he murdered my father. We've come to settle the score. But now you tell me he died?"

"Yes!" The banker pointed at his desk. "My father

was sitting at this very desk one afternoon when he just keeled over and was gone."

The beautiful woman shook her head in disgust. "There's no justice in this world. I wanted to see your father beg for his life before I shot him to death like he did my father."

The bank manager swallowed hard. "Miss, you . . . you aren't going to kill me instead of my father, are you?"

The woman's gun was aimed at Charles Bodney's heart. "If it's true that the apple never falls far from the tree, then perhaps I should kill you. You must have heard the old saying, like father like son?"

"No! Please! I never knew anything about where my father got all his money."

"Liar! You must have known he got rich selling a California gold mine." Sierra Sue's face hardened. "Don't stand there and lie to me, or I'll blow a hole through your heart!"

"Wait!" the banker pleaded, throwing up his hands in supplication. "All right. All right. I *did* know that my father struck it rich in the California gold fields when he was a young man and a forty-niner. But I swear I knew nothing about him stealing a mine claim and murdering anyone. That's the truth, I swear that it is."

She studied his face, and noticed that tears were streaming down his cheeks. "Charles, are you a married man with family?"

"I am! I have a lovely wife and two small children. Please don't kill me."

"Your father sold the California mining claim for thirty-eight thousand dollars," Sue told the trembling banker. "It was a fortune all those many years ago and it's still a fortune."

"I'll gladly pay you for the claim," the banker said quickly. "I've got that much cash in the vault and it's all yours."

"Plus interest."

"Yes!" he cried, sweating profusely. "Of course plus interest."

"Plus money for the pain and suffering my mother and us kids went through without a husband and father. Charles, while you grew up a rich boy, my mother had to work her fingers to the bone to keep us kids fed, clothed, and all alive. She died last year before her time, and I blame it all on Charles Bodney. All of our suffering I blame on your murdering, thieving father!"

Sierra Sue's voice shook with fury and the gun in her hand began to jump around in her fist.

"Name your price!" Charles Bodney II cried. "Please don't kill me! Name your price and it's yours for the taking."

"My brother and I want the full value of that gold strike plus interest. We want forty-eight thousand dollars."

The banker licked his lips, and then reluctantly nodded his head. "I will do that. Do you want it in gold or cash?"

"Cash will do." She reached out and grabbed her saddlebags, then emptied them of rocks across the banker's desk and plucked a single gold nugget from the pile. "This is the only gold nugget we had, so I'm keeping it."

"It's yours!" The terrified young banker stared down

at the pile of rocks and dirt that littered his beautiful office desk. "Is there anything else you want?"

"I want a written apology, a letter that states that you are sorry your father murdered my father and stole his mining claim."

"But . . . but I don't know that to be true," the man blurted out.

"Oh, it's true all right," Sierra Sue vowed, cocking back the hammer of her pearl-handled pistol. "And you'll be writing that letter now or you'll be seeing your father in hell."

"Okay! Okay!" he cried. "I'll write the note."

The banker sat down at his desk, pushed aside the rocks, and wrote the letter on his own handsome bank stationery. When it was finished, the woman read it carefully, and when she was satisfied, she said, "Now let's get that money you and your father owe us."

Charles Bodney II couldn't move fast enough to open his huge vault. Inside, there lay a fortune in gold, cash, and coin, but Sierra Sue would not take a cent more than the forty-eight thousand dollars she and her brother believed to be owed to them.

When the cash was stuffed into her saddlebags and her mission was finished, she said, "Your father was a backstabbing, murdering sonofabitch. I hope you didn't turn out to be just like him."

"I . . . I'm honest. I swear that I'm honest and a good husband and father."

"So you say." She took a deep breath and extracted a hundred dollars from the saddlebags. "There are two dead friends of mine lyin' out there in the lobby on your polished stone floor. No one except your damned father was supposed to die today . . . but things that weren't planned happened."

She laid the hundred dollars on the banker's desk. "See that those two get a decent burial and what money is left is put toward payin' the doctor for patching up that tall and handsome United States marshal I had to pistol-whip."

"What if you killed him?"

Sierra Sue shook her head. "If I did, that was not my intention. He was a gentleman, and those kind of men are hard to find. If he comes around like I'm hoping, tell him I am sorry for what I had to do. But there just wasn't any other way."

"I'll tell him."

"See that you do." Sierra Sue patted the banker's letter, which she'd neatly folded and placed in her pocket. "This forty-eight thousand dollars probably doesn't mean all that much to a rich man like you. But let's be clear about one thing before me and my brother leave this bank."

"I'm listening to whatever you say."

"If you send the law on our tail, then I'll make sure that your letter gets published for everyone to see so they know that your father wasn't the 'pillar' he was made out to be, but instead a murdering thief."

Charles Bodney II vigorously nodded his head. "I fully and completely understand."

"Then understand one thing more," Sierra Sue told him. "If you put the law on our tail, I will find a way to return and kill you. Once that's done, then your wife and kids will know the same suffering and pain that my family had to bear."

"I . . . I'll think of some way to try and keep the law from coming after you."

"Just tell them you don't know my name. Nothing else. And no bounty. No reward. Nothing!"

"You have my word," the banker vowed. "This conversation is our own personal secret."

"Now you've got it," Sierra Sue told him, heading out the doorway toward the lobby.

"Let's go," she said to her brother, who had his gun trained on everyone.

"Did you get what we came for?" he asked.

"I did."

"But you didn't. . . ."

"The old man died two weeks ago of heart failure," Sierra Sue explained. "So I didn't get to kill him."

Her brother swore in anger and frustration. "Sue, it's like I always told you since we were kids. There ain't no damned justice in this stinkin' world! No justice at all!"

Sierra Sue bent down and examined Longarm's head. "I hit him harder than I should have."

"Is he still alive?"

"Yeah, but he needs a doctor, so let's get out of here and let these people take care of themselves."

"What about Jed and Rowdy?"

She studied the two dead men that she'd brought into this mess. "They weren't much good and would have died by the gun on their own. But I did give the banker's son burial money for 'em."

"That was thoughtful of you, Sue."

"It was the least I could do for 'em," she said, touching Longarm's pale cheek and then turning to leave.

"Anyone comes outside and calls for help, we'll gun

them down in the doorway," the young man warned everyone else as he followed his sister outside.

Moments later, the two were riding hard out of Denver and they had no intention of ever coming back.

Chapter 2

Longarm awoke slowly and wondered where he was and what had happened. He tried to sit up, but Dr. Wilson placed a hand on his shoulder and cautioned, "Take it easy, Custis. You've been out for three days and we weren't sure that you'd ever come back. You've got a severe concussion."

"Yeah," Longarm groaned. "I see double everything. Where am I?"

"Miss Ellie Lander insisted that we bring you to her room so that she could take care of you. Your boss, Mr. Vail, also volunteered to keep you at his home until you recovered. But I decided that you might be happier and get more attention from your fiancée."

"My what?"

"Your *fiancée*, Miss Ellie Lander." The doctor frowned. "Can you remember anything from your past?"

He rolled his heavily bandaged head back and forth on his pillow. "When I try to think, it hurts and my mind is kind of foggy."

"Foggy?" The doctor raised his eyebrows with a look

of concern. "I suppose, given the gravity of your injury, that's not to be unexpected."

"Glad to hear it."

The doctor placed a stethoscope on Longarm's chest and listened to his heart. "Custis, do you even remember what happened to you?"

Longarm closed his eyes because seeing two versions of the same doctor was very disconcerting. He struggled to remember, and found he just could not. "I . . . I don't remember anything hardly."

"Your last name?"

"Maybe it's Long."

"Excellent!" The doctor put away his stethoscope and studied the heavy bandaging around Longarm's head. "And what is your profession?"

There was a pause. "I'm a United States marshal."

"Very good!" The doctor beamed. He was a short, rotund man in his fifties, bald as a billiard ball and round-shouldered, with muttonchop whiskers and penetrating gray eyes. He patted Longarm on the shoulder. "Given what you've just told me, I'm confident that you will retrieve much of your memory in its own good time. You can't force these things, and it may take months or. . ."

When the doctor didn't finish his sentence, Longarm felt alarmed and blurted out, "Or what, Doc?"

"I'm afraid that your memory might never come back in its entirety," the doctor said. "You suffered a very, very bad concussion. There was swelling on your brain, and I thought I might have to do something drastic like drilling a hole to relieve the pressure and drain any accumulated blood in your cranium. Unfortunately, the last time I had to take such measures, my patient never regained consciousness. It was very sad . . . and quite messy."

"I'm glad you didn't open up my skull," Longarm said, touching his face. "Was I shot in the cheek?"

"You were, but it was only a flesh wound. You'll have a permanent scar there, but I've discovered that you have quite a collection of scars. Knife scars, bullet scars, and scars that I can't even identify."

"I think I've probably led a dangerous life," he said.

"Of course you have. You're a federal marshal and you are quite legendary in Denver."

This was news to Longarm. "I am?"

"Oh, yes. And do you remember what happened at the Bank of Denver last Wednesday morning?"

"Nope."

"You were in a shoot-out with four bank robbers. You killed two of them, but I'm afraid that the other two escaped with quite a haul."

"How much?"

"According to the bank president, Mr. Bodney, a woman and her accomplice made off with sixty thousand dollars in cash."

"That's one hell of a lot of money!"

"It sure is. Young Mr. Bodney has been paying your medical bills, which I very much appreciate. He's as generous and kindhearted as his dear, departed father."

"I'll have to thank the man next time we meet."

"Charles Bodney has come by to check on you several times," the doctor said. "Along with your boss and some of your coworkers. And Mr. Bodney has offered a five-thousand-dollar reward for the capture of the woman and a man that we think is her brother. I can already tell you that your boss has put a good man on their trail, and I've heard that the bounty hunters are going out in force. I may be an optimist, but I am confident that they'll catch that pair, and I'd bet my money that they'll kill them dead and bring them back draped over their saddles for that huge reward."

Longarm was beginning to suffer from a monumental headache, but he wanted all the information he could get concerning the bank holdup and the person who had nearly busted his brain. "You say a *woman* was involved in the bank holdup?"

"That's right, and she was quite the looker, so I'm told. Black hair, buckskin breeches, and beaded leather shirt, all topped off with a pearl-handled pistol. The townspeople who saw her ride in on a palomino say she's a real Calamity Jane, only a whole lot better-looking. Do you remember anything about that woman?"

The pain was so intense it felt like someone had picked up an ice pick and was stabbing his brain. "No, afraid not."

"Here," the doctor said, giving him a bottle. "This will help with the headache. Drink the whole bottle."

Longarm gratefully swallowed the pain medication, not even asking what it was, but only caring about how fast and how well it worked.

The doctor continued. "Some witnesses said that you spoke to the beautiful woman both inside and outside of the bank. And I've saved the real kicker of this story for the last."

The pain medicine was acting fast. Maybe it was laudanum. "Give it to me straight, Doc."

"She's the one that pistol-whipped you so hard, she split your skull nearly in half."

"Is that a fact?"

"It is." The doctor grinned as if the idea of a pistol-whipping by a woman was something funny.

"What do you find so amusing?"

"Oh, nothing, Marshal. It's just that you have such a wicked reputation as a ladies' man and this beautiful bank robber was almost your final undoing."

"How about that," Longarm said, feeling damned irritable all of a sudden. "Anything else you can tell me?"

"No. I've heard the story secondhand, but I'm sure that Mr. Bodney will fill you in on the details the next time he comes by to check on your health. Despite how things turned out for you, everyone in Denver is calling you a hero for gunning down those two bank robbers in a stand-up shoot-out. Although there are a few that are saying you should have waited until they exited the bank so as not to put the customers inside at such a terrible risk."

"We all make mistakes, Doc." Longarm was feeling sick to his stomach. "Doc?"

"Yes?"

"I need a basin to vomit in. Whatever you just gave me is having a brawl in my belly."

"I got one right here," the doctor said, handing him a bucket. "Custis, you're going to be quite sick and dizzy for weeks, maybe even months. And about that memory loss? I'd just give it time and we'll hope for the best."

Longarm tried to answer, but then his gorge was coming up and he forgot what he had meant to say as both his stomach and the world started spinning totally out of his control.

"Custis? Custis, can you hear me, honey pie?"

Longarm awoke, not knowing how long he had been out in his fog. The room was now in evening shadows, and there was a large, soft woman lying naked by his side. She didn't smell good, but he probably smelled a whole lot worse.

"Custis, honey, you were talking crazy just now," she said. "I was worried that you were having some kind of a nightmare." The woman cradled his lean and muscular body next to her own pudgy body. "I sure have been worried about you, honey pie. I've been so worried, I haven't been able to eat or sleep since they brought you here to my room."

"Who *are* you?"

"Why, I'm your sweet and loving bride-to-be," she said. She nuzzled his neck and slipped a bare leg across his crotch, and at the same time stuck her hairy armpit right into his face so that Longarm felt his stomach churn.

"I don't remember you."

"I know. The doctor said that your memory is lost, but that you'll probably get some of it back. I don't care because I love you and I'm your darlin' fiancée, Miss Ellie."

He rolled his head to one side and away from her armpit so that he could at least breathe. "We're getting *married*?"

"We sure are. I've got a preacher waitin' and now that you're able to say, 'I do,' I'm callin' him in first thing tomorrow morning so he can make us man and wife!"

"Whoa up a minute here," Longarm said, his mind desperately groping to get out of the fog. "I don't re-member *any* of this."

"Well, that sure can't be held against you, darlin'. I guess you don't remember that you got me pregnant and we're going to have us a baby."

"A baby!"

"Yes, darling, *our* little baby."

Longarm tried to get out of the bed, but Ellie was too quick and the next thing he knew, she was on top, kiss-ing him and pushing him down into the soft feather bed so deep, he'd have had to have a shovel to get out.

"Ellie, hold on here!"

"No," she purred, taking his rod in her hand and then slipping down his chest and taking it into her mouth. "You hold on because I'm going to show you what kind of a wife I'll be for you, Custis."

Longarm tried to protest . . . a little. He tried to push her head off his manhood . . . but not really. And then he was remembering something real clear . . . how good it felt. The next thing he knew, Ellie had him inside of her and she was riding him like he was a brain-dead stallion. Her pleasure and excitement was awful damn conta-gious, so Longarm decided he might as well enjoy him-self seeing as he'd gotten the woman pregnant and she was going to have his baby.

"Oh, my gosh, Custis! You sure ain't forgotten how to do me!"

"Nice to hear it," he grunted as she pounded herself up and down on his stiff member until they were both crowing and hooting like roosters and owls.

Longarm let Ellie have all that he had to give, and when she finally stopped moving and lay quivering like a beached whale, he said, "Are we going to live here in this room?"

"Why, yes, Custis. I've moved all your things from your own rooms, and we're settled in here just as tight as ticks on a fat dog."

"Do you . . . do you work?"

"I did work as a waitress at the High Country Café, but since you got hurt so bad I quit my job, and we'll be able to make it on your salary until you find something that pays more."

"Oh."

She kissed his face all over, even pushing up the bandage. "I sure will be glad when they take this damned turban off your head and I can run my fingers through your long hair and see all of your handsome face."

"Yeah, that'll be good. But about getting married, Ellie."

"Don't worry! The preacher said he could do it with you lyin' down right here in our bed. You don't even have to get up or dressed or any damned thing. Just smile, say, 'I do,' and slip the ring over my little finger."

She giggled and showed him a little silver ring. "It didn't cost much and there's no diamond, but I know that you'll be good to me and the diamond will come someday. A real big one!"

"Mind rollin' off me?" he asked. "I'm kinda struggling for air."

"Sure, honey lamb." She rolled off him and farted, then got up and peed in a chamber pot. "How about a drink, sweetie pie?"

"I could sure enough use one."

"You remember what we drink, don't you?"

He took an easy guess. "Whiskey?"

"That's right! *Lots* of whiskey."

In the faint moonlight, he saw Ellie Lander grab a bottle and then slop two water glasses to the brim. My Gawd, he thought, she's *really* big and fat! Probably been pregnant for a while.

"When is our baby coming?"

"Oh, it'll be a while, darlin' of mine. And you'll make a good daddy, won't you?"

He couldn't even imagine fatherhood, but knew she wanted to be reassured, so he said, "I guess I'll give it an honest try."

"I'm not worried about that at all. Your boss thinks that you'll make a full recovery and go back to your usual duties."

Longarm took the glass from his fiancée, and then gulped down some of the fiery whiskey and immediately began choking. "Jeezus, Ellie. What kind of rotgut piss is this!"

She looked hurt; her porcine lips formed a pout. "Honey, that's your favorite drink, Old Bust Head."

"Old horseshit is what it tastes like," he said with a grimace.

"My, but we're feeling kinda finicky this evening, aren't we? Well, I guess I can understand that some things are just going to take time. But drink up, sweet'ums, and after that glass, you'll think that Old

Bust Head is the best tastin' whiskey you ever swallowed."

"I will?"

"Sure you will. And I'll let you in on another little
surprise."

He tried not to scowl. "To be real honest, I'm about
all surprised out, Ellie."

She ignored his remark. "When we're through with a
little drinkin', I'm gonna do you all over again just like
we did before!"

"You mean. . ."

She jumped off the bed and did a little dance while
flapping her ponderous breasts. Longarm suddenly remembered that he had once seen a dancing circus ele-
phant.

She turned away and gave him a full look at an ass as
wide as that of a Missouri mule. Then she turned back
and cooed, "Custis, honey, I'm gonna show you a few
tricks that I learned in the trade."

"What *trade*?"

Realizing she'd made a slip of the tongue, Ellie threw
her chubby hand up to her mouth, then said sweetly,
"Never you mind. Let's not go into our pasts, sweetie
pie," she admonished with a giggle. "We're going to be
married in the morning and our little baby is bakin' in
my lovin' oven."

It took Longarm a moment before he realized what
she was saying. "Well, if the little jasper is in your oven,
maybe I shouldn't be puttin' my meat loaf in with him."

Ellie Lander threw back her head and laughed like a
braying Belgian draft horse.

"What's so funny?" he demanded.

"Well, Custis, putting your meat loaf in my hot little oven has never been a concern for you before. And maybe it's a good thing that you're making your baby's acquaintance a little before the rest of us."

Longarm considered that and decided it was not a pretty picture, so he took another long slug of Old Bust Head and lay back on the bed with a deep groan of resignation.

Chapter 3

"Custis! Custis, wake up!"

Longarm awoke with a start and stared up at his boss
and good friend, Marshal Billy Vail. "What. . ."

"Ellie Lander is on her way to get a preacher! Are
you crazy!"

"What do you mean?" he managed to ask, head
throbbing from a vicious hangover coupled with the
pain from his concussion.

"What do I mean?" Billy threw up his hands in exas-
peration. "Why would you ever marry a whore and a
hog like Ellie?"

Longarm groaned and closed his eyes. "Billy, I got
her pregnant and I'm going to do right by her and our
baby."

"*What* baby!" Billy Vail was almost shouting. "You
stupid fool! Everyone in town knows that Ellie has had
her eye set on you for months and that she's no more
pregnant that I am!"

Longarm blinked. "You sure, Boss?"

"Of course I'm sure. Ellie got drunk night before last

and admitted that she was just fat and not pregnant. But she's going to get you hitched and then you'll be no good to me, yourself, or anyone else."

Longarm pressed his hands to his temples and tried to sit up, but the room started spinning. "Oh," he moaned, "I'm not sure if I can get up, much less fight off Ellie and a marriage-minded preacher."

"I'll help you out of here, but we have to hurry," Billy said. "Ellie is bigger and stronger than I am and I sure don't want to wrestle that woman to save your hide."

Billy helped Longarm crawl out of bed, and then got him dressed in a haphazard fashion.

"Where's my gun?" Longarm asked groggily.

"I got it at the office along with your badge. Now let's get out of here quick before Ellie and the preacher show up!"

Billy was considerably shorter and smaller than Longarm, but so great was his panic to avoid a confrontation with Ellie Lander, that he hoisted Longarm up and got the big lawman's arm draped over his narrow shoulders. "Come on, let's move!"

But they were too late. Ellie and Preacher Alvin DeWitt met them at the door, and for a moment there was just a stunned silence.

"What in the hell are you doin' to my Custis darlin'!" Ellie screeched, trying to grab Longarm.

"I'm taking him out of here and you can't stop us," Billy said, putting his body between them while trying to keep Longarm erect. "Now step aside, woman."

"The hell I will!" she shrieked. "That's my husband that you're trying to steal from me, Mr. Vail."

"He's not your husband yet, and if I have anything to do about helping my friend and best marshal, Custis never will be your husband."

"Now wait just a minute here, Marshal Vail," the preacher stammered, his face reddening. "This man has agreed to marry this woman and be a father to his child. God has joined this pair in blood and soon in spirit, and no man shall put that bond asunder."

"Bullshit!" Billy raged. "They're no more bound in blood or spirit than I am with my dog. And this . . . this woman . . . has publicly bragged that she is not pregnant, and even if she was pregnant, she regularly sleeps with so many low-life men that only God himself could sort out the true father!"

Ellie's eyes widened with outrage. She drew back her meaty fist and threw a punch that missed Billy, but hit Longarm instead on the point of his jaw. Longarm's legs folded and he was knocked out cold.

"Oh, my Gawd!" Ellie cried, falling to her knees and cradling the unconscious Longarm. "I might just have killed him! Get him back in my bed! Get the doctor!"

Billy tried to pull her away. "*You* get the doctor, Ellie!"

For a moment, the big woman wavered with indecision, and then Billy snapped, "Go on, find Dr. Wilson, and you better pray that you haven't killed Custis Long or you'll be going to prison."

Ellie jumped up and thundered down the hallway.

"Do you really think he's dead?" the preacher asked, looking down at the unconscious Longarm.

"I think he'll wish he was dead if he wakes up and finds that you married him to Ellie Lander."

"But I. . ."

"Shut up and help me carry Marshal Long to my house up the street," Billy snapped.

"But. . ."

"I'll pay you whatever Ellie would have paid for the marrying!"

"All right then," the preacher said, bending over and helping Billy get the finest marshal in Denver to his feet. "Let's get movin'. I sure don't want Ellie to catch me helping you get him away from her."

"Amen to that," Billy said, grunting as they half led, half dragged Longarm out of the building.

A week later, Longarm was still recovering at Billy Vail's house, and feeling well enough that he was grateful for his boss saving him from becoming a husband.

"I sure don't know how to thank you, Boss. I was in such bad shape that I wouldn't have stood a fighting chance that morning against Ellie and the preacher."

"Well," Billy said grudgingly, "you've saved my bacon more than once, and you're far too good a lawman to be duped into marrying a woman the likes of Ellie Lander."

"Is she still trying to get to me?"

"Yeah, but I've posted one of my marshals at my door when I'm away so that she can't reach you. Ellie hates me with a passion and has gone on quite a tear in the local saloons. She kicked the crap out of a young fella that had the foolishness to call her a swine and a whore."

Longarm breathed a deep sigh. "I sure came close to

getting my balls crushed in a vise. I don't know how in the world I'll ever repay you for this one, Boss."

"Just get well and get your memory back. I really want to know more about the woman and the man who robbed the Bank of Denver."

Longarm thought hard, but came up with nothing. "I'm sorry. I'm trying to remember things, but they're coming back real slow."

"What *do* you remember?"

"I remember I have a yellow tomcat and my own rooms."

"I'm feeding your tomcat and he's fine. I left your window open a crack so he just comes and goes as he pleases."

"That was always Tiger's way," Longarm said, relieved that his cat was not starving.

Billy frowned. "How is it that you can remember you have a cat, but you can't remember you were in a gunfight and what that bank robber woman looks like?"

"Beats the hell outta me."

Longarm's large and bulky head bandages had been replaced by a much smaller bandage. His ears weren't ringing so much now, and a sudden movement didn't bring his stomach to a boil as it had earlier. Still, if he moved his head real quick, he got dizzy and sometimes even saw double. But he was improving each and every day.

"Boss," he said, "why don't you tell me everything that you know about the robbery, and maybe that will help me remember some of the details that you aren't aware of."

"All right, I will." Billy sat down beside Longarm and told him everything he knew in his usual concise and precise fashion. One of Billy's best attributes was that he was brief and to the point, never windy. Billy finished by saying, "So that's it. The pair of bank robbers made off with what Mr. Bodney says was sixty thousand dollars."

"That's one hell of a lot of cash," Longarm said. "Do Bodney and his bank officers have any proof that they lost that amount in the holdup?"

"No," Billy said, "and that could be a problem. I spoke to one of the bank officers privately, and after I swore not to identify him, he told me that the Bank of Denver *never* kept that much cash in their vault."

"So do you think that Bodney inflated the amount that was stolen?"

"Why not?" Billy asked. "If he thinks that he can keep the extra money for himself, I suspect he might have inflated the amount."

"That would be embezzlement and it would send Bodney to prison," Longarm said.

"Sure it would! But just like Bodney hasn't been able to come up with any proof of the amount of cash that was stolen, so we can't come up with any proof that he is lying."

"So how will it all sort out?"

Billy scowled. "I've asked our office in Washington, D.C., to send me its two best bank examiners. They're on their way to Denver by train and after they arrive, they will spend days, perhaps even weeks, going through all the volumes of the bank's records of disbursements, expenses, and deposits to see how much cash they were carrying in their vault the day of the robbery."

"They can do that?"

"They said that they could," Billy replied. "This would not be the first time that a bank manager tried to inflate the amount of a holdup and pocket the difference. And to make sure that there is no skullduggery, I've confiscated all the Bank of Denver's records and files so that they cannot be destroyed, altered, or lost."

"That must have sent Charles Bodney the Second through the roof of his father's bank."

"It did. But I have the right to do it, and so I did," Billy said with firm conviction. "I know that the senior Bodney was thought by many in this community to be able to damn near walk on water, but I always felt he was a little shady. That something just wasn't quite right with the man and he was not to be fully trusted."

"Hmmm," Longarm mused. "That's interesting. Has anyone picked up the trail of the pair that got away?"

"No," Billy said with obvious irritation. "It's like they just vanished into thin air. I've been told by witnesses that you and the beautiful bank robber had a short conversation outside the bank. Custis, can you remember what you talked about with that woman?"

"Not really. I can't even remember her face."

"Then you really did have some serious brain damage," Billy said. "Because she was apparently such a good-looker that anyone who saw her would never forget her face and her figure. So we have already interviewed a good number of witnesses who could identify her and the handsome young man who we think was her brother. But unless they are found or spotted some-where . . . well, we really have nothing."

"That's why you want me to recall what we might have talked about outside the bank."

"Exactly."

"I'll keep working on it, Boss."

"Do that. The robbery is almost two weeks old, and even that five-thousand-dollar bounty has not produced a single clue as to who they are or where they went with the cash."

"They must have been seen by someone after they rode out of Denver. And if the woman was so beautiful, she would be remembered."

"That's what I keep telling myself," Billy said. "But they've still disappeared like a pair of ghosts. We've got to find them."

"Do you know what kind of horses they were rid-ing?"

"Yes. The woman rode a fine palomino mare and the younger man a bay gelding. The two that you shot dead had bays as well, and we have them at the stable."

"No clues in their saddlebags?"

"Nothing. Nothing at all," Billy said, sounding dis-couraged. "There's a lot of pressure on me about this case, and I sure wish we'd get a break."

"The doctor has me up walking a bit now," Longarm said. "I think I'll be able to ride a horse in a couple more days."

"No, you won't," Billy said. "I've talked to Dr. Wil-son every day, and he says that it will most likely take six months to a year before you are physically back to your full strength. And he doesn't know if you'll ever regain your complete memory."

"I will," Longarm vowed. "And it won't be any six months or a year before I'm able to go after that pair that robbed the bank."

"That's the spirit!" Billy said, brightening. "I sure could use you back in the field on this case."

"I'll be there," Longarm promised. "I was able to read a little bit of the newspaper you gave me this morning. The written words are coming back and it won't be long before it'll all come back to me."

"That's what I want to hear," Billy said. "My wife is cooking a pot roast tonight. How does that sound?"

Longarm couldn't exactly remember what a pot roast tasted like, but he didn't want to see Billy's disappointment, so he said, "It sounds just fine, Boss."

When Billy left a few minutes later to go back to his desk at the Federal Building, Longarm got dressed and walked out of the house and into the alley. He took a deep breath and began pacing the length of the alley just as he had been doing for the last two days. He was getting stronger, but it was painfully and discouragingly slow. He didn't remember a hell of a lot about his past, but he knew that he had always been a powerful man. Well, he wasn't anymore, but he made up his mind to change that fact.

"Next week, I'll ask Billy to drive me out of town and I'll take my pistol and start practicing. Maybe I lost my memory, but not my aim."

Longarm hoped that would be the case. He could see that Billy was under a great amount of pressure to find the bank robbers, and he wanted to ease that pressure by finding the pair just as soon as he could.

"A beautiful woman that I chatted with and then she almost scrambled my brains like a pan of breakfast eggs," he mumbled to himself as he began pacing unsteadily back and forth in the littered alley.

Chapter 4

By the time the two federal bank examiners arrived from Washington, D.C., Longarm was back in his own rooms with his yellow tomcat. He was feeling pretty spry, although he still had occasional dizziness and headaches. Little by little, he had started to remember things that had happened the day of the bank robbery. And he even thought he recalled some of the conversation he'd shared with the female bank robber concerning the cold, cold waters of Lake Tahoe.

"The freezing temperature of Lake Tahoe? That's an odd thing to have struck up a conversation about," Billy offered. "Did the woman actually say she was from Lake Tahoe?"

Longarm shrugged. "I'm not sure. But I think she said she was from there and that her name was Sierra."

"Sierra?"

"Yeah," Longarm said unconvincingly.

"No last name?"

"I don't think so. But I'm thinking that maybe there was some other name attached to Sierra."

They both sat in Billy's office pondering this mystery. Finally, Billy said, "Was her name Sierra Jane or Sierra. . ."

"It was Sue!" Longarm clapped his big hands together with delight. "Yep, Boss, I'm sure that she said her name was Sierra Sue."

"Lake Tahoe is in the Sierra Nevada Mountains," Billy said. "Odd name for a woman to go by. Maybe she was just tossing that out to put us on the wrong trail since she and the three men she rode in with were about to rob the bank."

"That makes sense."

"We've got a federal field office and marshal in Reno," Billy said. "I'm going to send him a telegram and ask if he's ever heard of someone named Sierra Sue fitting the description that we have of her."

"And if he has?"

"Then," Billy said, "I'll send Deputy Marshal Alston to Reno to investigate the case. He'll leave on the train first thing tomorrow morning."

"Hubert Alston couldn't even investigate a missing mutt," Longarm groused.

"I know he's not real sharp," Billy admitted. "But he's all I've got until you're fit to travel."

"I'm fit to travel now," Longarm told his boss. "And maybe by the time I reach Reno, I'll have *all* my memory back."

Billy studied his favorite marshal. "If I tell Dr. Wilson that you are going after a pair of bank robbers this soon after your concussion, he's going to explode."

"Then tell the good doctor that you're sending me to Reno and Lake Tahoe for a vacation in the cool pines.

Tell him that a soothing, deep blue lake will be a tonic for me and the high clean air will most certainly hasten my full recovery."

"We have high clean air here in Denver."

"Well," Longarm said dismissively, "tell him whatever you think he wants to hear."

"Hmmm," Billy mused. "Give me a day or two to ponder this."

"What's to ponder?" Longarm asked. "I've been practicing with my gun and my aim and reactions are almost normal."

"Almost?"

"I still get headaches," Longarm admitted.

"Are you still seeing double?"

"Just a touch of dizziness when I turn my head too quickly."

"Hmmm," Billy mused again. "It might be all right. But first I'm going over to see Mr. Charles Bodney. The two bank examiners that came from Washington have given me an initial report about their audit, and it's rather disturbing."

"What do you mean?"

"I mean," Billy said, "that it seems that Mr. Bodney actually has inflated his bank's losses by at least ten thousand dollars."

"And they feel they can prove this fraud?"

"Yes." Billy paused a moment before continuing. "And I'd like you to be there when we confront Mr. Bodney about that supposed sixty thousand dollars in cash he says was taken from his bank's vault."

"Any particular reason you want me there?"

"The bank examiners say that, according to all the

evidence they can gather, the Bank of Denver could not have had more than fifty thousand dollars cash in the vault. That means Bodney is trying to embezzle at least ten thousand. I want you to listen to what the man has to say and then push him a little . . . make him angry and try to get him to make a mistake."

"You want me to grab Bodney by the shirtfront and shake him up a bit?" Longarm asked, still not sure of what was expected.

"I want you to do whatever it is that you think will work so that we can get at the truth."

"Bodney isn't going to admit to lying about the amount stolen without some real provocation," Longarm said. "He knows he could go to prison for embezzlement."

"That's right." Billy steepled his fingers. "You might just have to use some kind of . . . *extra persuasion*."

"If I attack Bodney, he might hire a lawyer to sue my shirt off and have my badge."

"Don't worry about losing your shirt or your badge," Billy assured him. "Short of beating the man up, I'll cover for you."

"You don't like the banker, do you?"

"No," Billy admitted. "And as I said before, I think his father was shady. Did you know that Charles Bodney the First had a young mistress in hiding for many years?"

Longarm's eyebrows shot up in surprise. "Old Charles Bodney the First had a mistress?"

"Yes. A lovely woman named Mary Hayden. She was young enough to be the senior Bodney's daughter and she lives on a farm outside of Denver. A small, very

poor farm. Her husband is an invalid, permanently paralyzed from the waist down by a horse he was trying to
break for the plow. Mary Hayden came to the Bank of
Denver ten or eleven years ago because her farm was
about to be foreclosed. She went to Mr. Bodney and
begged for an extension for her loan. She told him that
the farm was all she and her disabled husband had in
this world, and taking it away would kill her husband,
a proud and good man. Mr. Bodney refused to extend
the loan unless Mrs. Hayden was willing to offer him
certain 'special services.' And having no choice, she
agreed."

Longarm was fascinated by this account. "And what
happened to Mrs. Hayden after that?"

"The woman still comes into town once a week for
supplies. And she always stops over at the hotel for a
short one-hour 'rest.' Mr. Bodney was always absent
from the bank at that very same hour that Mrs. Hayden
needed her rest."

"So she serviced the rich old goat for ten or more
years, and then he died."

"That's right." Billy steepled his pudgy fingers and
said, "And two weeks after Charles Bodney the First
died, guess what?"

"What?"

"Charles Bodney the Second was taking the same
privileges as his late father."

Longarm's jaw dropped with surprise and disbelief.
"You mean Mary Hayden is. . . ."

"That's right. She is giving the old goat's son the
same services that she gave to his father once a week at
the Antelope Hotel."

Longarm shook his head in amazement. "That's quite a story. How come you never told me about this before?"

"What was the point? Mary Hayden made her choice long ago to do whatever she had to do to save her farm. She and her husband never had any children and she goes to church every Sunday. I know Mary and like her. She's still quite beautiful and I'd never want to hurt her or her husband."

"But you want me to threaten to tell everyone the truth?" Longarm asked, not understanding.

"Use the threat only as a last resort and as a bluff," Billy said. "I'm sure that would be enough to help Mr. Bodney recall the exact amount of money that was taken from his bank."

"You play real rough, Boss."

"So do you, Custis. And outside of a lying preacher, the next worse thing is a lying banker."

"I see what you mean," Longarm said. "And I'll play the hole card you've just handed me only as a last resort."

"Mrs. Hayden always comes into town on Wednesday. Her rest hour at the Antelope Hotel is at one in the afternoon until two. She stays in the same room, Number Two-fourteen upstairs. Mr. Hayden's health is very poor. If he discovers that his Mary is doing this to keep their farm, there is no telling what it would do to the man . . . and his wife."

"I'll make sure that doesn't happen."

"I know you will," Billy said. "Now let's get ready to go over to the bank and confront Mr. Bodney about the accuracy of his memory concerning how much money was *really* taken by the bank robbers."

"Ought to be very interesting," Longarm said, eager to get back into some challenging work.

"Tomorrow is Wednesday and if Banker Bodney doesn't fess up today, then you play that Hayden hole card tomorrow . . . but only as a bluff."

"I got it," Longarm said, climbing to his feet and preparing to leave with Billy Vail for the bank.

When Longarm and Billy walked into Charles Bodney's plush bank office, the two bank examiners were already seated and looking quite upset.

"Marshal Vail! Deputy Marshal Longarm! I'm glad you've finally gotten here!" Bodney snapped. "If I understand things correctly, these two fellows are accusing me of some impropriety regarding the bank's recent losses."

"Is that so?" Billy said, taking a seat and motioning for Longarm to do the same. "Why don't we hear exactly what they have to say?"

The senior federal bank examiner was a thin, balding man in his forties named Wilford Pence, and he nervously cleared his throat. "We have not accused anyone of theft or fraud," he said, addressing everyone in the room. "However, my associate and I have spent a great deal of time and effort examining all of this bank's records and . . . well, there is just no possible way that there could have been sixty thousand dollars in cash on hand to give to the bank robbers."

"That's ridiculous!" Bodney cried, pounding his impressive office desk. "This is a large and prosperous bank."

"I'm not saying that it isn't," Pence said, unwilling to back down in the face of the banker's fury. "But you absolutely could not have had that much cash on hand. Not even counting coinage."

Bodney pretended to be even further outraged. "Are you accusing me of lying?"

"I'm afraid that's the long and short of it," Pence said tersely. "And to be very candid, we are recommending that you personally be investigated and charged with perjury and theft."

"What!"

Billy Vail stood and said, "Take it easy, Charles. The truth always comes to light. I'm guessing that you simply miscalculated how much money was taken during the holdup. Perhaps you just made a mental miscalculation and overstated the amount by ten thousand dollars or so."

"I never miscalculate!"

Marshal Billy Vail smiled with cold intolerance. "I think, Mr. Bodney, that you ought to take a little time and recalculate the amount that this bank really lost in the holdup."

"And if I refuse?"

Billy looked young Charles Bodney right in the eye. "As these two expert bank examiners have just suggested, this could go very hard for you . . . and your bank."

"This meeting is over!" Bodney cried, jumping up from behind his desk in a fury.

The two bank examiners looked to Billy Vail, who

said, "Gentlemen, I have your findings and extensive written report. Marshal Long and I will take over this matter, and we appreciate your dedicated and professional service."

"It has been . . . difficult," Pence said, casting a hard look at the banker. "We've had very little cooperation from this bank or any of its officers, which we have duly noted in our report."

"I understand," Billy said, trying to smooth their feathers. "Now, good day, gentlemen, and we wish you a safe and comfortable trip back to the East Coast."

When the pair of bank examiners was gone, Billy shut the door and returned to his seat. "Sit down, Charles," he ordered.

The president of the bank was not used to being told what to do, but he sat anyway. "Marshal Vail, I have never been so insulted or humiliated. The very idea that that pair would question the accuracy of my losses! It's outrageous, and someone will hear about it in Washington, of that you may be sure!"

"So you can't be persuaded to . . . to reevaluate the figure of sixty thousand dollars in losses?"

"Of course not! Those bank examiners were idiots! Completely incapable of carrying out their assignment!"

"In that case," Billy said, turning to Longarm with a nod of his head, "I think our business is finished here today."

Bodney had obviously not been expecting the lawmen to leave his office so quickly, and he gave an audible sigh of relief. "Good day then."

"Good day," Billy and Longarm repeated as they left the bank.

"Well," Billy said when they were back on the street. "What do you think?"

"I think that Charles Bodney is bluffing, scared half out of his mind, and lying through his teeth."

"Of course he is. And tomorrow is Wednesday."

"Antelope Hotel, Room Two-fourteen at one o'clock," Longarm recited. "I'll be there."

"Have the hotel desk clerk give you a key to the room so that you don't have to wait in the hallway for an invitation."

"I hate to do this to Mary Hayden."

"She made her own bed. We have to protect all the bank's depositors."

Longarm nodded with reluctant agreement. "I wonder how much Mrs. Hayden still owes that bank on her farm's debt after all these years of servicing the old man and his son."

"I have no idea," Billy said, frowning. "But you might take the opportunity to *renegotiate* the loan amount."

Longarm grinned from ear to ear. "Billy, sometimes we are of a like mind."

"Custis, let me know how it goes tomorrow as soon as you have left the hotel, because your afternoon is sure to be a lot more interesting than my own."

Chapter 5

Longarm checked his Ingersoll watch, which was attached to a mean little double-barreled derringer. It was one fifteen on Wednesday afternoon, and time to pay a surprise visit to the Antelope Hotel. Minutes later, he walked into the hotel and up to the registration desk.

"I'd like a key to Room Two-fourteen," he said to the hotel desk clerk, whose name he remembered was Ernie Yankovic.

Ernie was a drunkard who was almost always incoherent after eight o'clock in the evening. Longarm had seen him in saloons or passed out on the sidewalk plenty of times, and there was talk that Ernie had been a mule skinner who had killed a man in a barroom brawl and had spent some hard time in prison. Yankovic had once been a big, strapping man, but prison, guilt, and cheap whiskey had reduced him to a shell of his former self.

"Marshal," the clerk said, "I'm afraid that Room Two-fourteen is currently occupied, but I could give you another room."

"No, thanks."

Ernie Yankovic swallowed hard and began to tremble. "But Marshal, I really can't give you the key to that room."

"Then I'll just take that extra one hanging on the hook behind you," Longarm said, coming around the desk and snatching it off the board.

"Please!" Ernie begged. "You can't go up there now. If you want the room, I can have it readied for you in an hour or two."

"Relax," Longarm said, suddenly feeling pity for the ruined former mule skinner.

"Marshal, if you go up there I'll lose this job, and I probably can't find another job in Denver. You know my reputation and history."

"Yeah, I know what you did and that you served your full time in prison. Ernie, don't worry about your job," Longarm told the frightened and now badly shaken clerk. "I'll see that you don't lose it. Now just sit down and relax, because you look to me like you're about to seize up inside and die."

In response, the thin, shaking clerk reached under the desk and grabbed a half-full bottle of whiskey. Without a word, Ernie pulled the cork and poured the liquor down his throat, spilling some onto his dirty shirtfront. Longarm gave the pathetic figure a sad shake of his head and said, "If I need you to be a witness to what is going on up there, I'll holler down the stairs. If you don't come running, I'll make your life even more miserable than it is already. Is that understood?"

"Yes."

"Good," Longarm said. "This won't take long and

you'd better not try and finish that bottle before I come back down. Understood?"

Ernie Yankovic solemnly nodded his head, and set the bottle firmly down on the registration desk.

Satisfied, Longarm started up the stairs, his mind troubled and at the same time excited. Troubled because of the shame he would bring to Mary Hayden, even if her secret tryst never became public . . . excited because he wanted to nail Charles Bodney II to the wall and break the arrogant sonofabitch like he would a rotten limb.

Room 214 was locked, as expected. Longarm gently inserted his key, and then he shoved the door open to discover exactly what he'd expected. Banker Bodney was naked, his fish-belly-white buttocks pressed tightly between the naked outstretched thighs of Mrs. Mary Hayden.

"Well, well," Longarm said. "Good afternoon, Mr. Bodney! Having a nice time?"

Bodney howled with shock and humiliation before he rolled off the married woman, his little pink pecker wet and glistening. Completely rattled and at a loss for words, he grabbed the covers and covered himself, amusing Longarm almost to the point of laughter. He would have laughed at the sight, except that Mary Hayden's eyes filled with tears and she began to sob, not even bothering to cover herself. And she was a good-looking woman still.

Longarm closed the door behind him and then locked it. He turned back to the bed to see Bodney peeking over the bedsheets in his direction, too mortified to begin his familiar cries of outrage.

"Bodney, I know what you and your father have done to this poor woman for the last ten years. How much has she managed to work off her mortgage debt to your bank?"

Finally, Bodney found his tongue. "That's none of your gawdamn business, Marshal Long! Now you get out of here or. . ."

"Or what?" Longarm laughed, a cold, hard sound. "Are you going to climb out of that bed with all your glorious manhood exposed and whip my ass? Or are you going to call the police and have me arrested?"

Bodney gulped and tried to push down the little tipi where his manhood was making a dying stand. "Marshal Long, please let's be reasonable here. Mary is. . ."

"Is a married woman," Longarm said, his voice turning as brittle as glass. "And you're a married man. A family man who goes to church every Sunday and puts a large and very public donation in the collection basket. So guess what the scandal will be when this news about you and Mrs. Hayden hits the front page of the newspaper?"

"You wouldn't dare!" Bodney cried.

"Sure I would." Longarm's voice softened. "Sorry, but I would, Mrs. Hayden."

It took her a moment to gather herself enough to wipe the tears off her cheeks and then whisper, "It doesn't matter. Nothing you could do or say could hurt me any more than I've already suffered. I'm a ruined woman. I deserve whatever happens to me."

"Don't be so hard on yourself," Longarm cautioned. "You did what you thought was the only way to save your farm. Your husband couldn't help you. The only one who could was the banker, who was prepared to take your farm . . . or let you work off the debt in that bed."

Mary did something unexpected. She reached over and backhanded Charles Bodney full in the face. She did it with such savage force that it broke the banker's nose and caused it to gush with blood. Then, she kicked him, rolling and wailing, out of the bed to the floor, where he curled up into a ball.

"Marshal," she said, "please draw that gun on your hip and shoot me through the heart."

"What?"

"You heard me," Mary said, climbing out of the bed. "Shoot me through the heart and then tell the town that I wanted to die because of my shame at having slept with this pig and his father, who was an even bigger pig."

"Hold on, Mary," Longarm said, holding up his hands. "I got a much better idea. And my idea is that Mr. Bodney here is going to write off all the debt on your farm and give you a free and clear deed to that property. And in return, no one will ever know about you and this room."

Bodney tried to protest, but his round face was covered with blood and he was weeping into his cupped hands.

"Mary," Longarm continued, "I've seen quite a few property deeds, and I've even had one drawn up and ready for Bodney to sign *right now*. I'll be the witness to his signature. If Charles tries to protest, I'll tell the editor of the *Rocky Mountain News* all about him and how he tried to cheat his depositors out of ten thousand dollars."

"No!" Bodney cried.

"Yes," Longarm said. "Charles, quit blubbering and wash your face with that towel and then sign over this deed to Mary and her husband, or I'll call the desk clerk, Ernie Yankovic, up here to witness the sorry spectacle you have always been despite your money and fancy airs."

Charles Bodney wiped the blood from his nose and sniffed like a hurt child. "This will be our secret?" he asked, almost in a begging voice.

"If you sign over the farm and confess to trying to cheat your depositors out of ten thousand dollars."

"Please, I can't do that!"

"You have no choice," Longarm snapped. "What is it to be, you pathetic piece of dog shit!"

Five minutes later, Charles Bodney was gone. Longarm watched the broken and soon-to-be-imprisoned banker stagger across the street below, holding his broken and bleeding nose.

"What is going to happen now?" Mary Hayden said. "When my husband hears about this, he will die of a broken heart."

"Unless you tell him yourself, there is no reason for him to ever know, ma'am." Longarm handed her the newly signed and witnessed property deed giving her free title to the Hayden farm. "You're finished and it's time for you to go home. No more Antelope Hotel for you, ma'am."

She took the deed and stared at it with fresh tears of gratitude. "Marshal Long, I . . . I don't know what to say."

"Go home and try to forget what you had to do for the sake of yourself and your husband."

"I'll never forget or forgive myself," Mary said, getting fully dressed and then quickly combing her long brown hair back from her face.

"You're still quite a beautiful woman, Mrs. Hayden," Longarm told her. "And a brave one on top of that. If I were your husband, paralyzed the way he is, and I found out what you had done to keep a roof over my head, I'd put you on a pedestal and make you a permanent shrine."

More fresh tears cascaded down the farm woman's cheeks. "You're a living *saint*, Marshal Long."

"Most people think I'm more like Satan," Longarm replied, managing a grin. "But I know true courage when I see it in a man . . . or a woman. And besides, you helped me break Bodney, and now he'll be facing charges of embezzlement and fraud for inflating the amount of money that was stolen from his bank."

"Will he actually go to prison?"

"I can't say because that will be up to a judge and jury," Longarm told her. "I will say that Bodney won't be the president of that bank after all the dust settles, and he won't ever be held up on high in Denver again."

"So he'll be ruined."

"Yes ma'am, he will be. And justifiably so."

"Like me."

Longarm went to the woman and took her gently into his arms. "Mary," he said softly, "only you know what you should do or say when it comes to your husband and what has been happening in this room all these years."

"It absolutely would kill Arthur to know what I've done on that bed."

"Then don't tell him."

"If I don't, someone else will."

"No, they won't," Longarm vowed. "I'll have a word with the clerk downstairs, and I'll scare Ernie so bad he might not ever drink again. And he'll know that he can never speak of you or Mr. Bodney and what went on in this room."

"So this really could be kept a secret?" she asked, a faint trace of hope in her voice.

"It can if you want it to be."

"Oh, I do! Arthur has been hurt so badly already."

"Then do the right thing and let's take this secret to our graves," Longarm said passionately. "Let's just swear to take it straight to our graves."

"All right," she breathed. "Let's."

Longarm stepped back. "If you weren't married, I'd be comin' around with flowers and candy to your farm."

"After what you know about me and have seen in this room just now?"

"*Especially* after what I know and I've just seen."

Mary Hayden blushed. "My, oh, my," she said, "but you are some kind of man."

Longarm chuckled, feeling happier than he had since the morning he'd been pistol-whipped by Sierra Sue. "Mary, you'd better get that deed to the courthouse and have it recorded before you go back home."

"I will."

Longarm started to leave.

"Marshal Long?"

"Yes?" he said, turning.

"Can I kiss you before you go?"

"Hell, yeah! If you'd like."

"I would," Mary told him as she came forward and gave him a kiss on the lips. Then, leaning back and looking into his eyes, she said, "That was a kiss to say thank you and good luck. And good-bye, because I don't think we'll ever be able to speak to each other again this way."

"I'm afraid we won't," he agreed.

"I'll never forget your kindness."

"And I'll never forget your courage," he said, leaving her there and heading downstairs.

He found the desk clerk and gave the poor, trembling man ten dollars, but also the warning never to tell a soul about what had taken place upstairs in Room 214.

"I won't, Marshal! I swear I won't!"

Longarm picked up the ex-mule skinner's bottle of whiskey, poured it on the floor, and left the hotel saying, "Ernie, if you quit drinking, you might even last another twenty or thirty years."

Chapter 6

In a dirty little saloon and former Indian trading post about eighteen miles northeast of Laramie, a gaunt and grubby sodbuster with a new hat and shirt named Homer Gray was buying drinks on the house . . . just as he had been doing for the past week.

"Drink up, boys! Drink up on old Homer Gray!"

And at the now familiar sound of this generous and boozy offer, a dozen or more cowboys, merchants, and other men eagerly crowded up to the makeshift bar and shoved out their glasses to be refilled thanks to Homer's newfound wealth and generosity.

Nobody knew much about Homer Gray except what he'd told them, how he'd sold his dirt-poor homestead up to the north of Laramie and south of Casper for more money than he'd ever dreamed.

"And the pair that bought it weren't even farmers!" Homer would crow every night to a chorus of drunken laughter.

"How many acres did you have, Homer?" a cowboy asked, leaning over the bar and pouring himself another drink from Homer's bottle. "Do ya suppose they could have been rich cattle ranchers?"

"Hell, no! There ain't much grass to speak of on my six-hundred-forty-acre homestead. Besides, how many damn cattle could you run on that little bit of rocky land with hardly no water?"

Homer always said the same thing, and it always got the same uproarious response and gales of drunken laughter.

"Well, then, Homer," a wizened trapper said, "if your homestead wasn't no good for farmin' and it weren't big enough for runnin' cattle, why'd you reckon they paid you so much for 'er?"

"Damned if I know!" Homer cawed. "I was drunk when they rode up and asked me what I wanted for the homestead, and I told 'em it'd take a thousand dollars! A thousand dollars for a piece-of-nothin' land and a barn and a cabin that I built so cheap that the walls fly off just about every winter in the high winds!"

More whoops and laughter.

"Are you gonna keep buyin' us all drinks until that thousand dollars is gone?" a blacksmith asked. His question brought frowns from the others, who didn't want Homer to be thinking about the fast-approaching time when he would have spent all his money at the Bear Claw Saloon.

"Well, I did save half the sale money. Got it buried out on the prairie where it can't be found by anybody but me. As for the other five hundred, I'm spending it on this whiskey, whores, and a hell of a grand old high time with all you friends. But I did treat myself to a few things. Why, I bought this here new shirt and hat, and I had a pair of boots made which ain't near as comfortable as my old work boots, but they sure are pretty. And I bought a new holster and pistol, too!"

Homer slapped the fancy hand-tooled holster and new Colt revolver on his hip, and said with a sloppy grin, "'Course, I can't hit the broadside of a barn with no pistol, but it sure looks fine hangin' on my side, I reckon! Makes me look like a real gunfighter!"

More laughter and slaps on Homer's back as the bartender grinned and kept pouring from the bottles of whiskey that Homer had bought for all his new friends.

"Homer, what you gonna do with the five hundred dollars you got hidden?"

Homer slammed his big fist down on the bar. His hands were big and calloused; he'd grubbed so long in the dirt that the grime could never be scrubbed out of the knuckle creases. Homer Gray was not an old man, but he looked old from all the years of hard work in the bright sun and strong Wyoming winds.

"Come on, Homer! What are you gonna do with that five hundred dollars!"

"Well . . ." Homer paused, tossing back another shot of whiskey and wiping his whiskery face with the back of his sleeve. He looked up and down the bar to make sure that he had everyone's full attention, and then he said, "Homer Gray is gonna buy a train ticket all the way to California, and then he'll finally see the blue Pacific Ocean."

"The ocean!" a cowboy said, making a face and almost choking on his free whiskey. "What the hell do you want to see some old ocean for!"

Homer just grinned and motioned for the bartender to

refill his glass. "Boys, I'm gonna maybe see if I can farm right on the beach and . . . and I'll fish, too, by Gawd!"

He tossed back a full jigger of whiskey, coughed, and added with a smile, "Yep, old Homer's just gonna fish and farm and fuck. That's all I'm ever goin' to do again until the day that I die. No more hogs to feed."

His eyes focused somewhere in the future, and the saloon grew quiet while everyone considered Homer's future. Then Homer added in an almost dreamy voice, "No more rocky fields to try and plow or grass to cut for winter hay. No more freezin' blizzards and no more bakin' sun and swarms of hungry mosquitoes." He shook his head as if feeling a great sorrow. "Boys, for me there will be no more tryin' to raise a few crops and a little runty corn. No more bein' cold and half starved and knowin' I'm workin' just to see another failed harvest. No, sir, none of that for Homer Gray no more because I'm sure as hell gonna start havin' fun fer a change. Just fishin', farmin', and fuckin'!"

Everyone stared at the worn-down sodbuster, and then they burst into laughter and slapped each other's backs as if they'd just heard the funniest joke ever told. And so another drunken and happy evening passed at the Bear Claw Saloon, and everyone sure hoped that Homer would forget about California and stay in Wyoming until every last cent of that one thousand dollars was spent on buying his newfound friends *whiskey*.

Several days later, three grim bounty hunters rode into town and happened to hear Homer's story about how a rich and either crazy or stupid pair had bought his miserable little homestead for ten times what it was worth.

"Did you hear that?" a tall, hatchet-faced former buffalo hunter named Cutter, dressed in bloodstained buckskins, whispered to his friends. "A couple of fools paid that dumb sodbuster a fortune for some worthless old homestead that wasn't worth spit. Why, I heard this last winter was so bad in this country that you can ride just ten miles north of Laramie and find homesteads abandoned for hundreds of square miles. The banks are still givin' 'em away for less than fifty dollars a section. I heard that the banks and the homesteaders who haven't just walked away from their land are beggin' buyers to give 'em anything for their land and buildings."

By far the biggest and scariest of the three new arrivals was named Mace. He had cruel, deep-set eyes and a full beard tangled with grease and grit. His voice was a deep rumble. "It's a shame that some fool like that Homer fella gets so lucky while we can't find head nor tails of the pair that robbed the Bank of Denver. Some dumb bastards have all the luck."

"Yeah," the third man, Jake Poole, agreed. "Maybe we could find a way to get that five hundred he says he still has buried somewhere."

"Maybe," Mace said, "the sodbuster is plannin' to dig up his money real soon so that he can take that trip to California. When he does, we could jump him and steal the five hundred."

"Why, Jake," Mace rumbled, motioning for the bartender to refill his glass on Homer's money, "that is the best idea you have come up with since we left Denver."

"Let's see if we can find out when the sodbuster plans to leave this shit hole and head for the train."

"Good idea."

So the three bounty hunters put on broad grins and shoved the working cowboys aside as they closed in on Homer like vultures on a dying dog. And since Homer's usual five bottles of whiskey only lasted until around midnight, they even bought a sixth bottle, just for themselves and for Homer Gray.

"So when are you leavin' on that train for California?" Mace asked, leaning over and laying a massive hand on Homer's thin shoulder. "'Cause, from the way you keep buyin' drinks for everyone, you just might not have enough money to buy a train ticket even as far as Green River."

"Oh, I'll have the money," Homer said, smiling stupidly and then ducking his head to whisper. "And don't tell all my friends here, but I'm fixin' to catch the train day after tomorrow."

Mace glanced over Homer's shoulder with a big smile, and then he said, "Is that a fact, Homer?"

"Yep. I've rented a horse and I'll be leavin' early tomorrow morning." Homer shook his head sadly and looked around the dingy saloon. "I sure am gonna hate to leave all my friends here at the Bear Claw Saloon. Nicest bunch of fellas I've ever known, and we sure have had a time of it, but I've gotta be moving on while I've got a little money left."

"Sure you do," Jake Poole agreed, nodding his head. "And the Laramie train station is only a half day's ride from here. Matter of fact, me and my friends are also goin' to Laramie tomorrow. We'll just ride along and keep you good company."

Homer slapped his hand down on Mace's big shoulder. "Why, you boys are just altogether fine gents! I'd enjoy your company and I'll be sure and pack a bottle or two of whiskey for the ride."

"We will enjoy that," Poole said, grinning. "A little hair of the dog will taste just fine tomorrow."

Homer drew all three of the bounty hunters in closer. "Don't tell all these new friends of mine that I'll be leavin' early tomorrow mornin'. They'd feel bad about it and I'd just as soon ride off with no sad farewells."

"Don't worry," Mace said, showing an almost toothless grin. "Ain't nobody but us gonna know about you leavin' for Laramie."

"I knew you three fellas could keep a man's secret," Homer said, grinning from ear to ear and hiccupping loudly. "I'll meet you just south of here come daybreak.

"One more round on me!" Homer Gray cried. "One more round on the luckiest man in this cold, windy, and godforsaken part of Wyoming!"

Dawn was just breaking over the eastern horizon when Cutter, Poole, and Mace mounted their trail-weary horses and rode south out of the settlement. They didn't say much to one another because all three had splitting headaches. When they topped a ridge, a cold wind was blowing down from the north and the faint outline of the Bear Claw Saloon, where they'd gotten drunk only hours ago, could barely be seen.

"We don't have to kill the dumb sodbuster," Cutter told his companions. "He's a good enough fella. After he digs up his money, we could just take his five hundred dollars along with his horse."

"I think we better leave him deader than a can of corned beef," Mace growled. "Because if Homer makes it back to the Bear Claw Saloon and tells all them boys how we did him so dirty, they're gonna want to come after us if for no other reason than to get Homer's five hundred back for drinkin' money."

"I agree," Jake Poole said sullenly. "If we steal the sodbuster's damn horse, money, new gun, and whatever else he has of worth, we're gonna be damned unpopular fellas in these parts. Those saloon rats will come after us like flies on shit."

Cutter scowled. "I suppose you are right, but I did kind of like the fool and I sure hate to kill the poor fella."

"Listen," Mace said, giving Cutter a hard and intimidating stare, "this morning is a cartridge-and-corpse occasion and I mean to see him planted without a readin'. It's the only way."

Mace glared at Cutter until he nodded. Then he said, "Jake, you're the best of the three of us with a gun. You do the honors."

"No, sir!" Jake protested. "If we're gonna agree to murder the sodbuster, then we'll all have a hand in it by Gawd!"

"Jake is right," Cutter said after a moment of silence. "We *all* have to put a bullet through poor Homer. We're all gonna have a hand in this, and we'll fill him so full of holes that the poor devil wouldn't float in brine. That way, if we get caught, we go down fightin' together or get hanged together."

Mace clearly didn't like this arrangement, but he could see his companions were not going to change their minds, so he nodded his shaggy beard in agreement. "All right then. We all shoot the poor bastard until our guns are out of bullets. Then we bury him shallow and then ride hard."

"His gun is new and I want it and that fancy leather holster," Cutter said. "And I hope Homer rented a good horse and saddle that we can sell for a lot of money in Laramie."

"As long as he has that five hundred dollars on him, we'll be fine," Mace said. "We're down to small change, and these horses are about worn out from all the huntin' for those bank robbers we been doin'."

Poole offered, "Boys, if we get the five hundred, maybe we should just forget about the bounty and ride on down to Santa Fe for some Mexican girls and tequila."

"Sounds good to me," Cutter replied, brightening.

"Me, too," Mace rumbled. "But we gotta have the five hundred because the pretty señoritas ain't gonna give us nothin' in Santa Fe for free."

"Here comes Homer now," Cutter said, checking his gun. "This is gonna be like shootin' ducks in a barrel."

"Let's get him a few miles away so nobody in the settlement hears our gunfire," Poole said, touching spurs to his thin horse and putting a frozen grin on his lean face.

Homer Gray was clearly suffering from a hangover, and his happy smile and genial nature were missing when he came up to the riders. "Boys," he said. "I do recall us planning to ride to Laramie. Glad you remembered."

"You're our friend, Homer," Mace said. "We want to make sure that you get to Laramie and on board the train to California without being robbed of all that money you dug up this morning."

"Yeah," Homer said, "I got it dug up. But no one would hurt me because everyone in these parts is my friend. I've bought 'em drinks and we've all shared laughs. I ain't gonna miss trying to farm in these parts, but I sure did like the men who live here. Salt of the earth, that's what they are."

"For a fact and you're a generous and good-hearted man," Cutter said to the sodbuster. "And we mean to take care of you."

"Thanks, boys," Homer told them. Then he leaned far out of his saddle and emptied his belly. He wiped his face with his sleeve and groaned. "I'm gonna sleep on the train all the way to the Pacific Ocean, and I ain't gonna get drunk on whiskey for a while. My guts feel like they've rotted all out."

"I don't expect you will drink any more whiskey," Mace said through his matted beard. "No, sir, Homer, I can guarantee that you will never get drunk again."

Mace's two companions shot him a warning look, but Mace ignored them, and they all started toward Laramie with the sun coming up to warm their weary and weatherworn faces.

"I gotta take a piss," Homer said about an hour later as he reined his rented horse up and leaned over his saddle horn, holding his belly with one big hand. "And, boys, I think I'm tossin' my guts again."

Cutter, Jake Poole, and Mace stayed mounted. They exchanged long glances as Homer Gray dismounted and then sagged to his knees and began to vomit.

"Let's let him finish and stand on his feet and face eternity like a man," Cutter whispered to his companions.

Mace and Poole nodded and watched as Homer retched repeatedly. When the sodbuster finished, he struggled back to his feet and clung to his stirrup for support. "Boys," he said, shaking his head with regret, "I swear to you that I ain't never drinkin' so hard again."

"I'm afraid you got that right," Mace said, drawing his gun and pointing it down at the sick and gasping sodbuster.

Homer must have heard Mace's change of voice because he raised his head and saw all three of his new-found friends had their pistols out and pointed at him. "Homer," Cutter said, "we're sorry that it has to be this way, but we're dead broke and at least you've had some fun in the end."

"Boys," Homer choked out, suddenly turning even paler than he had been a moment before. "What . . . what are you doin' with those guns! You're my *friends*, ain't you? I bought you whiskey! Lots of whiskey and now . . . now you're plannin' to do me a terrible wrong?"

"We need your five hundred dollars real bad," Cutter said when Mace and Jake Poole looked away in shame. "Homer, get it out of your saddlebags or wherever you hid it."

Homer's eyes filled with tears, and they began to roll down his sunken cheeks. "You're gonna rob me of all my train and California money! After what I done for you and all, you're gonna rob me?"

"It's hard times we're livin' in," Jake Poole said with a sigh. "And we sure do need that money."

"But it's mine and I got it from sellin' my homestead to this pretty woman and. . ."

Cutter was thumbing the hammer back on his pistol and taking aim when he suddenly froze. "Did you just say that a pretty woman bought your homestead?"

"Yeah, but. . ."

Jake Poole blinked. "Homer, was that a black-haired woman riding a palomino mare?"

Homer looked from one cruel face to another, and his voice trembled when he answered. "Yeah, but. . ."

"And," Jake went on, "was that pretty black-haired girl ridin' with a young handsome fella that seemed more like a brother than her husband? And did he ride a tall bay horse with three stockings?"

"That's right," Homer said. "But why do you have to steal my hard-earned money?" Homer was pleading now. He tore off his new hat and placed it over his chest. "Boys, I'm beggin' you not to steal all my homestead money! I bought you drinks and called you my friends. Don't take my money or my. . ."

Homer Gray couldn't bear to say what was most prominent in his terrified mind. That they might even have plans to shoot him down and also steal his life.

Mace raised a big hand to silence Homer's pleadings, and now he was focused on getting a five-thousand-dollar reward, or maybe even more. "Sodbuster," he rumbled, "tell us exactly where we can find this homestead you sold to the black-haired woman and her brother. And I mean tell us *exactly* where we can find your farm."

"Why, sure!" Homer said, hope surging back up in his long face. "Why, you just ride straight north about forty miles and you'll come to a river. Well, it's really more like a stream."

"There are a lot of streams in this part of Wyoming," Jake Poole allowed.

"This one is real pretty," Homer told them. "And just to the east of it is a bluff that looks like a sailin' ship, only it's out there in the middle of nowhere. And there are some tall pines stickin' out of the side of the bluff. You'll know it when you see it."

"Go on," Mace growled.

"Well, about two miles past the bluff, you'll see my soddie and an old fallin'-down wood barn off to the west. It's set back against a low, red cliff, and you'll see my fields fallow with nothin' but sagebrush and weeds. And there's a broke-down wagon near my soddie. You can't miss it. Can't miss it even if you tried."

"Any neighbors around?"

"Nope," Homer said, hanging on to his stirrup and feeling sick again. "There ain't nobody around there anymore. "Mr. and Mrs. Hyam and their kids had a place about. . ."

"Shut up," Mace hissed. "You're talkin' too much."

"Where's the five hundred?" Jake Poole demanded. "Get it out now."

"Oh, please, take some, but not all of it."

Homer tore open the flap to his saddlebags and dragged out a thick stack of bills. He split the stack and extended it to the three horsemen saying, "I just want to see the Pacific Ocean. I always wanted to see it and I need enough to buy that one-way train ticket. And then some money left to buy a little farm with good dirt. Just a small farm overlookin' the Pacific. It's all I want in this whole world. A small California farm and a one-way train ticket."

"I'm afraid the only one-way ticket that you're getting is to the Promised Land," Mace said, cocking back the hammer of his pistol and motioning to his friends that it was killing time.

"No!" Homer screamed until the sound of gunfire drowned out his dying voice. Cutter, Jake Poole, and Mace emptied their revolvers into Homer Gray. They sent him flying back away from his rented horse with his big, calloused hands flapping at the sky as bullet after bullet tore through his body.

When the sound of the gunfire fell silent, Cutter shook his head and began to reload. "Kinda hated to do that to the sodbuster. But we had no choice. If he'd have gotten back to the Bear Claw, they most definitely would have come after us like flies on shit."

"Or if Homer had made it to the train in Laramie, he'd have gone to the marshal there and they'd have come after us for stealin' his horse and money," said Jake. "Either way, we'd be the hunted instead of the hunters."

"And now we know where to find the bank robbers,"

Cutter said, as he dismounted and unstrapped the new holster and pistol from Homer's bullet-riddled body.

Mace got down and collected the money that had fallen from Homer's fluttering fingers, while Jake Poole went through the sodbuster's pockets collecting coins, a barlow pocketknife, and a good-luck charm.

"We need to bury him."

"I got a little shovel head in my pack," Mace said, looking north into the lonely country. "You think anyone back at the saloon and trading post heard all our gunfire?"

"Naw," Poole said. "Too far."

"We sure shot the shit outta the poor, dumb bastard," Jake Poole solemnly observed.

Mace took the shovel head out of his pack and went over to what looked like soft, wet ground. "I'll start diggin' the hole. You boys will finish it and cover him."

"Messy work," Cutter said. "I never seen anyone bleed so much as Homer Gray."

"I never seen anyone take that many bullets. I hit him with all six."

"Me, too."

"Same here."

"So he's got eighteen bullets in his body," Poole said. "Why, boys, we put more holes in the fool than a cabbage leaf in a hailstorm."

They all forced a laugh at this poor attempt at humor, but didn't laugh very hard. Fifteen minutes later, they were riding off with an extra horse to sell and a newfound purpose.

Now, at long last, they knew exactly where to find

the woman and her brother and the thousands of dollars they'd taken from the Bank of Denver. And they sure as hell had no intention of handing it over to a Denver banker for a measly five-thousand-dollar reward.

Chapter 7

Sierra Sue and her brother Bob sat on a rough bench in front of Homer Gray's humble soddie and relaxed as the sunset fired up the red cliffs. A nice breeze stirred in the budding cottonwoods and a red-tailed hawk soared overhead. It was June, and the grass and weeds were coming to life for the short summer ahead.

"Sue?" Bob asked, whittling on a stick. "How much longer do we have to stay here in hiding?"

"The longer the better," she answered. "You know there will be a big reward on our heads and every bounty hunter in Colorado and Wyoming is probably out looking for us."

"I know," Bob said, whittling steadily, "but we've been here nearly three weeks and we haven't seen a living soul. I'm going stir-crazy, if the truth be told."

"We've got to stay put until the heat dies down," Sue told her twenty-year-old brother. "And we've got to find some different horses."

"I could go looking for 'em," Bob volunteered. "I could go first thing tomorrow. We've sure got the money to buy replacements. I could ride down to Laramie and be back in two days with some real good horses."

Sue smiled because she knew how hard the waiting was on her kid brother. Bob was friendly, a flirt with the ladies and a handsome fella everyone liked to be around. He could talk and talk all day and hardly say anything worth hearing, but he was a sweet and kind brother and Sierra Sue loved him dearly. But Bob's sociability was also a liability in a situation like this when they were being hunted. If he had been a homely and unfriendly sort, she would have felt more comfortable sending Bob out for some badly needed supplies and a change in horseflesh. But her gregarious brother would get to jawing with folks, and pretty soon he'd say something that might get both their necks stretched or a bullet sent from a bounty hunter's gun into their brains.

"Come on, Sue!" Bob pleaded. "We're down to moldy bacon and beans. Flour is gone. Coffee is gone. Sugar is gone. Why, I'm so hungry I could eat a sow and her nine piglets and then go after a boar hog for dessert."

"Just another few days, Bob."

"We can't make it another few days," he complained. "Not unless we eat our horses or the bark off them cottonwoods."

"I'll go out and see if I can get an antelope first thing tomorrow morning," Sue promised.

"I'll go with you," Bob said, tossing what remained of his whittling stick into the yard. "At least, shootin' an antelope would be a distraction from the boredom around here."

"I'd rather you stayed close to this soddie," Sue told

her brother. "The bounty hunters are looking for two people. That's why I need to ride your bay horse tomorrow and leave my palomino here with you, because she's likely to be recognized."

"Even if you do shoot an antelope," Bob said, "then we'll still be out of sugar, flour, coffee, and beans."

"Maybe I'll come across some homesteader or a trading post and buy all those things."

"And maybe pigs will fly," Bob groused.

Sue forced a smile. "Bob, we've had a plan from the beginning and we can't deviate now. We both agreed before we got to Denver that instead of running back to Lake Tahoe, we'd buy a cheap homestead and stay in hiding until late fall, and then work our way slowly back to California. Between now and then, bounty hunters and lawmen will be looking for us from Denver to Sacramento."

"I don't know if I can stand staying here until fall," Bob confessed as he folded up his pocketknife and stared into the vast emptiness that surrounded them. "It's only early June and you're talkin' another four or five months!"

Sue nodded. "At least that long. And even if we wait until October, there might still be lawmen and bounty hunters out there."

"Being stuck here is like being locked in a prison," Bob groused. "The soddie is like sleeping in a grave. Why, there are centipedes and worms galore that crawl out of the walls every night and onto our faces!"

"I know," Sue said. "I know."

Bob wasn't finished. "And when the rains come hard, the roof of this damned sod house leaks mud!"

"I know that, too," Sue replied. "I've never been on the Great Plains, but I've been told that a lot of poor farmers and their families live in these sod houses 'cause there's damn few trees to make lumber. I just can't see how a woman could keep a sod home clean. It'd drive me crazy living in one of these places year after year."

"It's driving me crazy already!"

Sue reached out and patted her brother on the knee. "Tomorrow I'll hunt us up an antelope and some wild onions to make a tasty stew. And maybe I will come across a homesteader or traveler and I'll buy some fresh supplies. Sugar and candy, too, if they have 'em."

Bob grinned. He was so easy to please, and one of the happiest people Sierra Sue had ever known under normal circumstances. But these sure weren't normal circumstances, and Sue understood that her brother was growing depressed. She wondered if, given his love of other people, he could actually stay with her in hiding until autumn without it affecting his mind.

"Sue?" Bob asked.

"Yeah?"

"Don't you think we should have shot that banker considering how his father cheated our father and led our parents to an early grave?"

"No, Bob, I don't. It wasn't the son's fault for what his father did back during the forty-niner gold rush days."

"I'll bet the son was as crooked as his old man," Bob said quietly.

"Even if he was, we aren't murderers. We were taught better than that," Sue replied.

"I would still like to go out tomorrow hunting antelope with you."

"And I'd really like to have you come along for the company," Sue told him. "But then I'd have to ride the palomino mare and, if any bounty hunters saw us together, they'd know in an instant that we were the ones that robbed the Bank of Denver."

"I guess you're right," Bob said, looking glum. "I guess I'll go down to the stream and see if I can catch any fish."

"That's a fine idea," Sue said, knowing they both understood that there were no fish in the little stream. But fishing was just a way to pass the slow time, and so Bob whittled a pole and tried it every few days.

Early the next morning, Sue got up and pulled on her buckskins and boots. She grabbed her rifle and strapped her pistol to her shapely hip, then went out into the pre-dawn light and fed the horses some grain before she gathered her gear and saddled Bob's tall bay horse. Light was just breaking over the red cliffs when she rode out from the soddie, not sure which direction would be best for hunting antelope.

There were lots of old buffalo wallows in this part of Wyoming, evidence that not more than a decade or two ago, there had been thousands of the free-roaming buffalo and plenty of Indians to hunt them for food and shelter. But the buffalo had all been shot for their hides, and the Indians had all been pushed onto reservations. The homesteaders who came to fill in the emptiness hadn't lasted very long. Free offers of land for the taking had brought hundreds of families to this country, but the long, hard winters, the poor soil, and the loneliness had driven them away until the land had nothing to offer anymore. Not to buffalo, not to free-ranging Sioux and Cheyenne, and not even to the optimistic but foolish homesteaders. Homesteaders who had broken their backs trying to eke out a living by farming, and then had had their hearts broken when not even their smallest dreams could be made to come true.

What remained now were just the vast canopy of blue sky, the grass, and some sweet-water streams. This was, Sue thought, a country meant for sheep and cattle and damned little else.

She decided to ride north this day, and she was in no hurry to shoot game and return to the soddie because Homer Gray's former homestead was a sad and depressing place. When they had first met Homer, she had seen the despair in the sodbuster's eyes, and the desperation, too. When she'd told him that she and Bob might be willing to buy his farm, the sodbuster had joyfully fallen all over himself like a puppy that had just been petted.

And when Homer Gray had asked a ridiculous price of one thousand dollars, Sue's first instinct was to laugh. But then she looked around and saw all the futility and labor that the poor man had put into the homestead, and the grave marker where his wife was buried, and she simply said, "Fair enough, Mr. Gray. We'll take it for one thousand dollars cash."

Sue smiled to remember how Homer Gray, hearing that she would pay him a thousand dollars, had almost cried with relief and joy. The man was so glad to be rid of his homestead, and the bitter memories that he saw every day, that he actually did a little jig in his front yard, and immediately looked about ten years younger.

As she rode along through the rolling grassy hills, Sue was thinking of these things and hoping that Homer was now basking on a beach beside the Pacific Ocean. It was a nice image in her mind, and it lasted right until she saw three antelope grazing in a low, grassy swale about a mile away.

She dismounted and took her Winchester out of its scabbard. Bob was a good horseman and he'd trained his bay well, so it was just ground-tied where it stood. Sue quietly levered a shell into the chamber and checked the wind direction. The wind was perfect, coming down from the north past the antelope and into her face. Antelope had excellent eyesight and were small and swift. They were hard to hit, but Sue wasn't concerned. She was an excellent shot with a rifle and with a pistol. Tonight, she knew as she dropped to her hands and knees and began to stalk the antelope, she and Bob would be feasting on fresh, red meat. Sierra Sue picked out the largest of the antelope, and knew that she would have to adjust her aim just slightly because the animals were about a dozen feet lower and her bullet would have to drop just a mite to make a clean kill.

Eight miles to the south, big Mace and his two companions, Jake Poole and Cutter, were barely in sight of Homer Gray's soddie and also stalking forward for the kill. They'd tied their horses behind some trees out of sight, and now they were moving in for a long awaited showdown.

"I'd kind of like to take the woman alive," Cutter whispered. "I hear she's a beauty and we could have some good times with her for a while before we have to kill her."

"Sounds like a fine idea to me," Jake Poole said in agreement. "I haven't had a woman in weeks!"

They both looked to Mace, who nodded. "We can pull straws for our turns on her," he said with a smile.

"There's the palomino," Poole said. "I wonder where the brother's bay horse went."

"Probably run away," Mace answered. "We'll sneak up as close as we can get. If they're still asleep, we can bust right through the door and grab the woman before she can run or grab a weapon."

"And just shoot her brother," Cutter said. "Ain't any good can come from keeping him alive."

"Best not to shoot him until we have that stolen money. They probably buried it someplace like old Homer did."

"You're right," Mace said. "We'll keep the kid alive until him or his sister has helped us get the stolen cash."

They all nodded at that, and paused to watch as a big coyote trotted intently through the grass on the trail of a rabbit not fifty yards in front of them.

The three heavily armed bounty hunters were moving fast now. They were in a running crouch toward the soddie. When they reached the yard, they didn't even hesitate, but slammed through the flimsy front door and into the dark and dank sod house.

Bob had been sleeping soundly, and when the bounty hunters burst inside, he was too groggy to act. One minute, he was dreaming of a pretty girl and a picnic beside

Lake Tahoe, and the next, he was being yanked out of bed and dragged into the bright morning sunlight.

"What the hell are you doing!" Bob yelled, struggling and fighting with all his strength.

Mace clubbed him to his knees with a wicked overhand to the temple. Bob's head exploded with pain and he nearly fainted.

"She ain't in here!" Cutter shouted from inside the sod house. "The woman is gone!"

Mace grabbed Bob by the hair and twisted his head back so violently, he almost broke the young man's neck. "Where's your pretty sister!"

Bob tried to tackle Mace, but the man's legs were like tree trunks and he wouldn't topple. Mace kicked him in the side, and Bob curled up in a ball fighting to stay conscious.

"Where is the money?" Jake Poole said, bending low to Bob's ear. "We don't want you or the woman that everyone is guessing is your big sister. What we really want is the bank's money. *All sixty thousand dollars.*"

Bob took a few deep breaths. He felt himself being dragged to his feet, and now he looked at the three men who had him captive. "Who the hell are you?"

Mace backhanded Bob across the face, splitting his lips. Bob spit blood and braced himself for more punishment. He was no coward, or so he hoped.

"One more time, kid. Where is the money and where is your pretty sister?"

Bob and Sue had buried the money in a coffee can about a quarter mile away. Buried it deep and covered it with dirt so that it could never be found except by themselves. Even in a sea of red pain, Bob understood that once these three had their hands on the money, he and Sue were as good as dead.

"It's . . . gone," he said, trying desperately to come up with some story that might save his life as well as that of his older sister.

"What the hell do you mean!" Jake Poole shouted. "How could it be gone?"

"We were robbed of it," Bob said quickly. "We were sleeping one night when two men found us, and then they took my sister and made her tell 'em where we hid the money. After she told them, they . . . they raped and killed her. I escaped. That's why my sister isn't here now."

Mace reared back and delivered a thundering upper-cut to Bob's stomach. Bob retched and bent over, suck-ing for air. Mace hit him again behind the ear, and Bob lost consciousness just as his bloodied face struck the ground.

"Dammit, Mace!" Jack Poole swore. "Why'd you go and knock him out cold? Who are we gonna ask to tell us where to find that bank money if he can't talk!"

"I don't believe his sister is dead. Look around for the woman," Mace growled. "Maybe she wandered off to take an early morning shit. See if you can find her tracks. As for this one, I'll wake him up soon enough."

"You be careful with him, Mace. If you break his neck or kill him, he sure ain't gonna be no help to us," Cutter warned.

"Go find the pretty woman."

Cutter and Jake Poole left Mace standing over Bob. Once they were out of sight, Mace went in and ran-sacked the soddie, tearing up two straw mattresses and all the furniture. He searched every inch of the sod house and came up empty, which did not surprise him in the least. Mace hadn't expected that the woman and her brother would be stupid enough to keep the money hidden inside the sod house. No, just like poor Homer Gray, they'd gone and buried it someplace.

"Damn!" Mace swore, going back out into the yard and standing over the unconscious kid. He used the toe of his boot to prod Bob, but that didn't wake him, so he found a bucket and went to get water from the stream.

Mace pitched the bucket of water on Bob just as Jake and Cutter returned.

"No luck," Jake said in anger. "She's gone."

"Any fresh tracks?" Mace asked.

"Someone rode a horse north away from here yesterday or this morning. Most likely early this morning," Cutter said, looking in that direction.

"That would be the sister," Jake Poole said.

"Most likely," Mace replied. "If it was, she'll be coming back, so get our horses hid up behind them cottonwoods."

"What about the kid?"

"We'll take him up in the trees, too, and make him sing like a gawdamn mockingbird," Mace vowed.

Jake and Cutter glanced toward the soddie. "You searched it high and low?"

"Yep," Mace answered. "Ain't any money in there to speak of. Less'n fifty dollars."

"We split that three ways," Cutter said. "We split everything including the bank money three equal ways."

"Sure," Mace snapped. "Now get our horses out of sight in case the woman is close and on her way back here!"

Jake and Cutter did as they were told. Mace grabbed the unconscious Bob by the arms and dragged him along behind him toward the trees. They would soon wake Bob up and torture him until he told them everything they wanted to know. Where the sixty thousand dollars in cash was buried and where his beautiful sister was and when she would return.

It would all be so damned easy, and profitable and fun.

Chapter 8

"Why, if it isn't Marshal Custis Long!" she exclaimed, putting her hands on her shapely hips and giving him a radiant smile. "I heard about you and that bank holdup. Everyone in Denver was talking about it a few weeks ago."

Longarm smiled at the receptionist who greeted people at the Denver Mint. He had spoken to her many times, but nothing had come of it, although he felt there was a strong physical attraction between them. He tried to remember her name, but like so many other memories erased by his severe concussion, this one just wasn't coming back like it should.

"Hi there," he said. "You're looking as lovely as ever."

She giggled. "And you're still the same handsome flatterer that you've always been."

"How's work going here?"

"Just the same as always. Pretty boring except when someone as big and handsome as yourself walks through the front door." Her smiled faded. "I'd heard that you were hurt pretty badly during that holdup."

"I got a skull fracture," he admitted. "But I believe I gave out better'n I received."

She smiled. "So I hear. You killed two men and probably saved a lot of innocent lives that day. I'm glad that you're back to normal."

"I'm still not quite back to normal," he told her, not wanting to reveal that he still had headaches and his memory was at times a blank slate. "But I'm working on it."

"Good for you, Marshal Long."

"Custis," he corrected, not even bothering to conceal his admiration for her shapely body and beautiful face framed with blond curls. "And I can call *you*?"

"Allison, but everyone just calls me Allie. *Miss* Allie Johnson."

Longarm pulled out his Ingersoll watch and looked at the time. "It's nearly five o'clock and I have just one quick call to make upstairs. How about as soon as I'm free I take you out to dinner, Allie?"

She didn't immediately say yes, but instead took a deep breath and thought about his invitation for a moment before saying, "I'd like that, Custis. Who are you seeing upstairs in this building?"

"A man named Peter Dunston. I understand he is in charge of currency distribution into the financial system."

"That's right. Is he expecting you?"

"Yes, he is," Longarm said.

"Mr. Dunston's office is Two-sixty-seven. Just make a right turn at the top of the stairs and go all the way down to the end of the hallway. When you're finished, I'll be waiting right here for you."

"That's great," Longarm told her. "And you can be thinking about what you'd like to eat."

Allie had bold, beautiful blue eyes, and she let them rove up and down Longarm's body. "I'll come up with something nice, but not so expensive it will bust your budget."

"That would be appreciated."

Longarm went to meet Dunston, a tall and agreeable-looking man wearing a pin-striped suit and sporting a handlebar mustache. Dunston got up when Longarm stepped into his office.

"Ah, Marshal Long!" he said with a warm smile and handshake. "Good to see you. Have a seat."

"Thanks."

"Marshal, what can I do for you?"

"I understand that you often put newly minted bills into the Bank of Denver for their initial circulation."

"That's right."

"Do you have a record of their serial numbers?"

"I do," Dunston said. "And I suppose you want them so that you can be sure that any monies recovered from the Bank of Denver robbery are in fact from that bank."

"Exactly," Longarm replied. "We need to have a list in the chief marshal's office."

"I will have a list there tomorrow morning. I understand that you took quite a bad hit on the head during the holdup from the woman bank robber."

"I did, but I have a very hard head."

"That would help in your line of work. Any reports yet of where the robbers went with all that money?"

"Nope," Longarm said. "It's as if they vanished into thin air. But I'm going to be leaving tomorrow on the train to start my hunt."

"From what I hear," Dunston said, "you are very persistent when you're on a manhunt."

"I don't give up easily. And given how much money was stolen, I have the authority to use whatever means I need to recover the money and make the arrests."

"Well," Dunston said, offering Longarm a cigar from a hand-carved wooden humidor, "it just amazes me that a woman as striking as the bank robber is supposed to be still hasn't been spotted, much less caught."

"She might have cut off her hair and pulled a hat down low over her eyes so that she could pass for a man. If she did, you can be sure that she is dressing in baggy men's clothing."

"Hmm," Dunston mused. "I hadn't even thought of that. Perhaps that is why none of the dozens of bounty hunters who took up the trail have yet to be successful."

Longarm leaned forward while Dunston lit his cigar. "Excellent tobacco," Longarm said, smiling.

"Cuban, of course," Dunston told him, obviously proud of his taste in cigars. "Cuban cigars and expensive Puerto Rican rum are two of my major weaknesses."

"They could have been a lot worse," Longarm suggested with a grin.

Dunston nodded. "Fortunately, I'm happily married and so my third weakness is no longer a problem."

"If it were," Longarm said, thinking he might find out a little bit about his upcoming dinner date, "I would think that you'd be after that lovely receptionist down on the first floor."

"Oh, yes!" Dunston chuckled. "But there is a very big complication when it comes to Miss Johnson."

Longarm leaned forward in his chair. "That being?"

"She has a very, very jealous boyfriend who is a quick-tempered blacksmith known for his violent nature."

"Hmm," Longarm said. "Have you seen this giant boyfriend?"

"I'm afraid that I have. Marshal, he even makes you look small. From what I hear, if he sees a man even looking at Allie Johnson, he goes into a murderous rage. So that's why everyone who knows about Allie gives her a wide berth despite her exceptional looks."

"Thanks for the warning," Longarm told the man.

"You weren't thinking of. . ."

"Actually," Longarm said, "that's exactly what I was thinking of."

"Marshal Long," Dunston warned, "you've just survived a terrible beating, and I'm sure that you're not fully recovered. That being the case, I would think that you would be wise enough to avoid a woman with a very dangerous and insanely jealous boyfriend."

Longarm puffed a smoke ring. "Mr. Dunston," he said, "I am a complete and unrepentant fool when it comes to a beautiful woman like Allie. I've invited her out to dinner tonight and she has accepted. Now, if she was married or even engaged to some fine man, then I might have a few misgivings. But a jealous boyfriend has no dog collar on Miss Johnson, and so she is free to go out to dinner with whoever she chooses."

Dunston shook his head sadly. "Marshal Long, I know your reputation both as a lawman and ladies' man and, frankly, I'm envious. But I just wish you would reconsider the dinner invitation and stick to catching whoever took the bank's money."

"Thanks for the advice," Longarm said. "I was thinking I might take Miss Johnson out to the newly opened Hillard's Steakhouse. Have you heard if it is any good?"

"It's excellent, but. . ."

"That's all I needed to know and I have full faith in your recommendation. And I know that those serial numbers will be in the chief marshal's office tomorrow. Just the large denominations will be fine."

"Have fun," Dunston said, "and if you get shot or beaten to death by the jealous giant, I'll tell everyone that you were warned."

Longarm nodded with understanding, and went downstairs to where Allie sat behind a desk. "Are you ready?"

"I am," she said, looking extremely nervous. "Let's go."

"What's the hurry?"

She snatched up her purse and her sweater. "I . . . I just want to get away from this building."

"Before someone shows up that might not be happy with me taking you out to dinner?"

Allie was pulling on a sweater, but now she stopped and looked into Longarm's eyes. "Mr. Dunston told you about Clyde."

"Yes. Why would you go out with such a man?"

"I don't go out with Clyde! I've never . . . never done anything with him, except once we got into a conversation and I guess I was nice to him. Ever since then, the man simply has not been willing to leave me alone." She

shook her head sadly. "I've tried to tell him I'm not interested in his attentions, but he refuses to listen. He gets
angry and I'm afraid of him."

"Don't you date anyone else?"

"No, because Clyde scares every man who even
gives me a second glance."

Longarm frowned. "You also look *scared*, Allie. Has
Clyde warned you not to date any other man or face the
consequences?"

"Of course he has," she said, looking away quickly.
"And he's not bluffing."

Longarm sighed. "Does he come by to pick you up
here every afternoon?"

"Almost every afternoon unless he's in a hot card
game or drunk. If that's the case, he'll show up at my
door later tonight."

"I see."

Allie put her hand on Longarm's sleeve. "Custis, I
know that you are a very strong and tough lawman, but
that won't matter at all if he sees us together. He will
come at you like an enraged bull and he'll hurt you very
badly. I think that maybe we should call off the dinner
plans."

"And I do what?" Longarm asked. "Walk away and
let you continue to be intimidated and scared by this
man who has made you his prisoner without actually
putting you behind bars?"

"You just don't know how big and mean Clyde can
be, Custis! I had a man your size once take me out
to dinner, and he was nearly beaten to death for his
trouble."

"Is that a fact?" Longarm said, folding his arms

across his chest. "The more you say, the more I want to meet this fellow and teach him a few of the harder lessons in life."

"You can't whip him in a fight," Allie warned. "You'd have to shoot him to death."

"Clyde would not be the first that I've sent to hell hopping over coals."

Allie was pale and shaking. Longarm bent over and kissed her lightly on the lips and said, "How about we have a steak at that new restaurant called Hillard's?"

"All right," she said, raising her chin with determination. "I'm a free woman and well over twenty-one, so let's do that."

The steak, potatoes, salad, and two bottles of French wine that they had shared, along with laughter and good conversation at Hillard's Steakhouse, were worth every penny that they cost Longarm. And that wasn't even the best part. Now, Allie was moaning with pleasure in Longarm's bed as he moved his manhood around and around stirring her juicy honey pot. This was the third time they had made love, and they had long ago lost track of time because they were so lost in their lovemaking.

"Oh, oh!" Allie cried, her back arching as her long legs trembled and she gripped him in a passionate embrace. "Oh, my heavens, Custis! I can't take any more of this tonight."

Longarm finished with a groan and sent the last of his seed into her coiled and lovely body. Then he rolled off the woman and sighed with contentment. "Allie, you are very, very good."

"And you, Custis darling, are the best I've ever had."

"I'd never tell that to Clyde," Longarm said. "That blacksmith sounds like he's got a few gears loose in his head."

"Oh, he definitely does," Allie agreed. "He's told me a few things about his own mother that would make your hair stand on end. I don't even want to talk about the man."

"All right," Longarm said, climbing out of bed. "We'll talk about a lot of things when I get back."

She stiffened at his side. "Back from where?"

Longarm gazed down at her face in the candlelight. "I guess I didn't mention that I'm leaving on the train heading west this morning. My boss thinks I'm well enough to go after whoever robbed the bank, and he wants me to recover the money. But I'll be looking you up the very hour I return to Denver."

"But. . ." She started to shake and couldn't finish her sentence.

"But what?" he asked, concerned by her reaction.

"If Clyde hears about us going out to dinner, he'll be so jealous I don't know what he might do. And if he even suspects that we made love three times, I'm probably a dead woman!"

Longarm rolled away for a moment and stared at his dark ceiling. "Where would Clyde be right now?" he finally asked.

"He owns a blacksmith shop over on Cedar Street. He sleeps in the back of the shop, but. . ."

Longarm kissed the terrified woman, and then he began to dress. Holding up his pocket watch to the candle's flame, he saw that it was almost four o'clock in the morning. His train didn't leave the station for Cheyenne for another five hours. That gave Longarm plenty of time to visit Clyde and either set the man straight . . . or send him to the cemetery.

"You aren't *really* going over to see him, are you?"

"That's exactly where I'm going," Longarm said, pulling on his boots and then reaching for his gunbelt.

"He keeps a shotgun at his bed."

"How do you know that if you've never slept with the man?"

"Clyde told me that he did. He told me that he's killed two burglars in the last five years. Shot them to death while they came into his shop to steal whatever it was they wanted."

"Thanks for the warning," Longarm said. "Does Clyde own a vicious watchdog?"

"No, because he hates dogs."

"That's a plus," Longarm told her. "Allie, stay right there in my bed and get a little sleep. That blacksmith shop isn't very far away and I'll return in time to take you out to breakfast before I have to catch my train."

Allie shook her head. "Custis Long, you're either stupid or the bravest man I've ever known."

"I prefer to be thought of as the bravest man you've ever known," Longarm said, leaning over and kissing her trembling lips.

Longarm made his way up the dark and cold streets brooding about how he was going to confront Clyde. If he had the time, it would have been far better to meet the giant during business hours and try to warn him away from Allie. If that failed, as Longarm expected that it would, then he could shoot the crazy bastard or at least send him to the hospital. But breaking into a man's place of business and living quarters in the predawn hours was another thing altogether. In such a case, Longarm knew that he would be committing an illegal act, and subject to going to prison himself if he shot and killed Clyde.

"Maybe I should wait until he opens his blacksmith shop," Longarm muttered to himself.

He decided that he would have to wait for Clyde to get out of bed, so Longarm passed the man's blacksmith shop and walked on until he came to a small café that was already open. He ordered coffee, biscuits, and bacon and was the first customer of the day.

By five thirty, the light was beginning to chase away shadows and Longarm was full and ready to face the jealous giant.

"Do you know the blacksmith that owns that shop just up the street?" he asked the man who poured him a third cup of coffee.

"Sure. Clyde has breakfast in here every morning."

"What time does he arrive?"

"He'll be along pretty soon now unless he was out late drinking. In that case, he'll be here about six thirty." The man studied Longarm for a minute. "You have some business with Clyde Hance?"

Longarm wasn't wearing his badge, so he simply answered, "You might say that."

"Clyde is usually in a pretty foul mood before he has his breakfast and pot of coffee. Are you his friend?"

"No."

"Then I can confess to you that I wish he would just drop dead. He scares away a lot of my other breakfast customers. Nobody laughs or talks much when Clyde is glaring at 'em. Yeah, he hurts my business all right, and I'm always wondering if he's going to go into a rage and beat me to death for serving him a breakfast that he isn't happy with."

Longarm said, "Why don't you just suggest to the blacksmith that he buy his breakfast at some other café?"

"Ha!" the man said bitterly. "You don't know Clyde at all, do you?"

"Nope."

"Well, if you did, you'd realize that you don't 'suggest' anything to Big Clyde Hance. Why, I heard a story about how he got mad at a Belgian draft horse that was dancing around and making it hard for Clyde to shoe. So the blacksmith threw down his hammer and punched the Belgian in the jaw! He knocked the huge beast to the ground and it was so stunned, the animal couldn't get back on its feet for five minutes. Clyde finished shoeing that poor horse on its side."

"Do you really believe that?" Longarm asked.

"Hell, yes! And you will, too, when you see Clyde."

Longarm nodded and he was beginning to think he should have brought a club or even a pickax to take on Clyde.

Almost an hour later than he normally arrived at the café, Clyde Hance slammed through the door, nearly knocking it off its hinges.

"Bring me my gawdamn usual breakfast and hurry up about it!" Clyde roared, pushing his way to a table. "And bring me a whole pot of strong black coffee!"

"Coming right up!" the owner said, shooting Longarm a quick and fearful glance.

Longarm took a deep breath and kept his head down over his own steaming cup of coffee. Clyde Hance was a monster! He had to be at least six feet six inches tall and three hundred pounds of muscle.

When the café cook and owner returned with a pot of coffee, he poured Clyde a cup and said, "Breakfast will be right up, Clyde."

"It better be."

As the owner passed Longarm, he leaned over and whispered, "Clyde must have got drunk last night and is feeling especially mean. I don't want your blood all over my place and I don't want the joint wrecked in a fight."

Longarm just nodded. He wasn't about to take on giant Clyde Hance in a fistfight because now he could see that would be suicidal. What he knew he should do was let the monster eat his breakfast, then leave, so he could be confronted on the way back to his blacksmith shop. But when Longarm checked his pocket watch, he saw that he needed to be getting ready to board the westbound train.

Longarm took a deep breath and stood up, laying money on his table. He placed his hat firmly on his head and stepped outside on the boardwalk for a moment.

"Holy hog fat!" he shouted, staring down the street, then bursting back into the café acting as if he'd seen a ghost. "The blacksmith shop is on fire!"

Clyde Hance came up from his chair so suddenly that he overturned not only his own table, but also the table next to him where two men sat quietly eating.

As Clyde rushed outside, Longarm stuck out his leg.

The giant tripped over the leg, and his momentum sent him diving off the boardwalk. Hance struck the dirt, skidded a foot or two, and then collided with a horse-watering trough headfirst.

Longarm seized the moment. He walked over to the prostrate giant and knelt beside the man, saying, "Clyde, I made love to Miss Allie three times since midnight. How's that square with you?"

Clyde was dazed, but he was able to roar like a bear and stagger to his feet. "You're the one she left the Mint with yesterday?"

Longarm took a step back. "Yep. And she says she don't ever want to see your ugly face again."

Clyde charged Longarm with outstretched arms. Longarm ducked under those giant arms and tripped Clyde to the ground again. "Clyde, before you go crazy, you'd better know that I'm a United States marshal and I'm either gonna arrest you for attempted assault on a federal officer, or else I'm gonna kill you. Your choice for breakfast."

"You sonofabitch!" Clyde screamed, scrambling to his feet and tackling Longarm before he could get out of the way.

They went down in the street fighting. Clyde grabbed Longarm by the throat with one hand and hit him so hard with the other hand that it sent all his senses some-where to the south of Old Mexico. Then Clyde drew a knife from his belt and hissed, "I'm gonna cut off your balls, Marshal! Cut 'em off and feed 'em to you right here in the street."

If the giant had instead decided to cut Longarm's

throat, it would probably have been the end of him. But instead, the jealously insane blacksmith made the mistake of trying to unbelt Longarm's holster and unbutton his pants.

"You crazy bastard!" Longarm snarled, pulling out the double-barreled derringer attached to his pocket watch and shooting Clyde twice in the face faster than a rattlesnake's venomous strike.

Clyde toppled over backward like a felled oak tree and his boot heels did a death dance in the dirt.

Longarm crawled erect and dusted himself off. He glanced over at the café owner. "Mister, did you just now see this giant asshole pull that knife and say he was about to cut off my balls?"

"I sure did!"

"When the local law comes, you tell 'em that Marshal Custis Long killed that big, crazy bastard in self-defense and you are more than willing to testify to that fact if necessary."

"I . . . I'll do that! *You're* Custis Long? The one they call Longarm?"

"At your service," Longarm told the man as he smacked the dirt and dust from his clothes.

"Well, you sure did me a service!" the café owner crowed, his face breaking into a wide grin. "And I am eternally grateful. Longarm, you come back for breakfast whenever you want and you won't have to pay me a red cent! Not tomorrow and not ever."

"I'll do 'er," Longarm promised. "You made a fine cup of coffee and the bacon was as good as I've had in a while."

The cook and café owner stared down at the dead giant as if transfixed. He said, "Glad you were happy with it, Longarm."

Longarm reloaded the derringer that was attached to his watch fob, saying, "Don't tell anyone about this little shooter attached like it is. I wouldn't want you to give away one of my professional secrets."

"No, sir!"

Longarm shook himself like a big stray dog and headed off down the street to see Miss Allie. Because Clyde had been so tardy, Longarm knew that he wouldn't have time to take Allie to breakfast, and he damn sure wasn't hungry anymore. But maybe. . . . just maybe, he would have time to make love to that lovely woman once more before he rushed to the train station and began to hunt for those two bank robbers.

Chapter 9

Sierra Sue dressed out her antelope, and was strong enough to finally drag it over and then lash it down across the back of her saddle. Her brother's bay gelding snorted and danced around, nervous with the scent of fresh blood filling its nostrils. Sue tried again and again to get the tall gelding to settle down so that she could mount up and return to the soddie, but that proved impossible because of the fractious animal.

"All right then, dammit, I'll walk back to the soddie, but you're still going to carry that bloody antelope."

In reply, the gelding snorted and danced around her in circles.

It was mid-afternoon when she wearily topped a low grass ridge and paused to catch her breath. Off in the distance, she saw the soddie and her palomino mare waiting in a little pole corral, but Bob was either indoors or off somewhere and not to be seen.

Sue started down from the ridge, still a good mile

from the soddie when she suddenly pulled up with the feeling that something was amiss. Perhaps it was because her mare was staring intently at a thick stand of cottonwood trees where a spring flowed from the hill. What was the palomino so interested in back in the cottonwoods? A bear? No, that wasn't possible. Then maybe another horse? Or . . .

Sue froze with sudden alarm bells going off inside her head. She was dog-tired, but all her senses were alert, since she knew that bounty hunters and lawmen were out hunting for her and her brother and all that stolen cash. Sue absently licked her chapped lips and squinted, trying to see even more clearly. She decided that she should just retreat behind the ridge and wait until she saw her brother and felt that everything was fine, with no bad surprises in hiding.

"Come on, horse," she said, pulling it around and moving quickly back behind the ridge. "Let's hold up for a while."

The bay wasn't at all happy about turning away from the soddie and corral, where it thought it belonged. The horse began to buck and fight Sue, and when she tried to grab its bit, the gelding reared up and broke free.

"Damn!" Sue swore as the horse with the antelope carcass went flying down the ridge and across a little valley toward the sod house. "Dammit anyway!"

Sierra Sue had a Colt revolver resting on her shapely hip, but the rifle that she had used to kill the antelope was flopping around in her saddle scabbard, and that unfortunate circumstance just might prove to be fatal.

Out here in this vast and open country, a pistol wasn't going to do her a hell of a lot of good.

Up in the cottonwoods, Mace, Cutter, and Jake Poole watched the bay gelding come racing toward the homestead.

"What do you make of it?" Mace asked the other two.

"Pretty obvious, I'd say," Jake Poole replied. "The woman shot and gutted an antelope and tied it on the back of that runaway horse. The horse was spooked by fresh blood, got loose, and came back here where it was fed last."

All three men turned their eyes toward the ridge that Sierra Sue was using to shield herself from their sight. Finally, Cutter said, "There is no telling how far that horse has run. The woman might be ten miles away from us. She might have gotten thrown from the horse and is badly hurt or even dead with a busted neck."

"That's true," Jake Poole said. "And we ain't getting anywhere with the kid telling us where they hid all that holdup money."

"I doubt," Mace added, filled with his own thoughts, "that the woman sent the horse on ahead just to see if it drew us out . . . but maybe she did. Do you boys think she might have somehow figured out we're waiting to grab her?"

"I don't see how," Cutter answered, his brow furrowed, "but I'm damned tired of hiding in these woods. What do you think we ought to do?"

The three bounty hunters considered the question for a long time before Mace finally decided. "We can't sit

here in these cottonwoods all day. We've done everything but shoot the kid, and he still won't tell us where
the bank's money is hidden. So that means that the
woman has to be taken alive and made to tell us."

"Maybe she can't be made to talk either," Jake Poole
said.

"Oh," Mace vowed with a wicked grin, "I can make a
woman talk every time. Make no mistake about that!"

The other two chuckled, and Jake Poole rotated his
pelvis until they both laughed outright. Mace had a terrible reputation for being hell on women. If he said that
he could make this one talk, they believed him.

"Here's the way I see it," Cutter said with a grin.
"The woman couldn't have known that we're hiding
here waiting to grab her. And there is no reason she
would have turned that bay horse loose with fresh meat
hanging off its back. So that means the horse either just
got away from her, or else she was tossed and is probably hurt."

"Either way, she'll be out there afoot and it'll be all
three of us against her," Mace reasoned. "I say we go
follow the bay's tracks to where the woman is and then
make her talk. But one of us has to stay here to watch
over the kid so he don't wake up and cause us grief."

The three exchanged glances. Jake Poole said, "I
ain't being nursemaid to the kid. I want the woman!"

"Me, too," Cutter said.

"Too bad," Mace said, hard eyes raking both of his
companions. "I'll go for the woman, and you two can
draw sticks about which one stays here with her brother
and which one goes with me to do whatever we need to
do to make her talk."

Minutes later, the sticks were drawn, and Cutter had to stay with the bloody and semiconscious Bob. Cutter was furious at being left behind, and he stomped off deeper into the cottonwoods swearing and kicking dead leaves. "By the time Mace and Jake Poole finish with her, there won't be enough left for me to have any fun with," he groused aloud.

Mace and Jake Poole rode out from the sod house at a gallop, following the bay's trail toward the distant ridge. The sky was like blue glass, flat and shiny, without a cloud and with very little wind. It was late afternoon and the sun was sinking into the western horizon. The prairie grass was young and a pale green color, and there was such a great sea of it that ten thousand buffalo could have fed within a rifle shot of the soddie for an entire month.

Crouched behind the ridge, Sierra Sue saw the pair coming at a hard run. She noted how one of the riders was huge and sloppy in his saddle, and how the other was slender and an excellent horseman. Sue had a few precious minutes to think, and she knew instinctively that her brother was either dead, or close to it. These weren't lawmen that had come to arrest her and Bob and take them to jail. No, these men were a far worse threat because they were bounty hunters, and they'd want the stolen money far more than any piddling reward.

The overriding question in Sierra Sue's mind as she lay flat just behind the ridge was how to kill the two oncoming riders with her short-range pistol.

She unholstered the revolver and studied it, as if the weapon had a mind and a will of its very own that she could bend and shape to her bidding. Sierra Sue was drop-dead accurate with a rifle, but with a pistol she was less than a marksman. The two horsemen that were obviously following the bay's tracks from the soddie had most of their attention directed toward the ground, which she understood was at least a small advantage. But they both had rifles in their saddle scabbards and if they weren't killed immediately, they would be able to grab their rifles, dismount, and kill her at their own chosen firing distance.

"I have to kill them both with this pistol," she told herself out loud. "And then I have to get one of their rifles and go see if poor Bob is still alive."

Sue closed her eyes for a few precious moments, and she could actually feel the earth tremble under the onrushing hoofbeats. She knew by the sound of the two horses' labored breathing that the riders were getting very close. Less than a hundred yards away . . . still too far for a certain shot from her Colt revolver.

Hold steady! Hold steady until their horses are almost on top of you! That is your only chance of killing them before they kill you.

She removed her Stetson and swept back her long black hair, feeling her heart hammering in her chest as if it wanted to escape by bursting through her rib cage. And when the sound of the hard-running horses seemed almost on top of her, Sue sat up, laid the pistol and her hand on a knee, and took a steady and deliberate aim.

The giant on horseback seemed to spring from the grass and soar over Sue's head to blot out the sky. In an instant, Sue understood that she would not have a clear shot at the giant, so she did the only thing she could and that was to shoot his horse through the chest. The racing animal somersaulted end over end, and the giant crashed to the grass rolling.

Sue twisted and fired two shots at the second horseman, knocking him out of his saddle. He also rolled on grass, and she continued to fire from her sitting position in a steady and unhurried way, until she saw blood spurts erupt from the smaller rider's throat and chest.

The gun out of bullets, she twisted around to see the giant staggering to his feet, eyes wild, face a smear of grass and bright red blood. He started toward her, dragging one leg. Sue tore fresh bullets from her gunbelt and reloaded; she was so frightened by the terrifying spectacle of the bloody giant that she dropped several bullets into the tall grass. Knowing there was no time to hunt for them, she tore two more from her gunbelt and managed to get them loaded. She snapped up the gun's barrel just as Mace threw himself on her in a bloody rage and roar.

The sound of her Colt's discharge was muffled as the giant slammed down on Sierra Sue like a rock slide. The giant's hands groped for her throat, and Sue twisted just enough to give herself shooting room. A second bullet tore into the giant's body and she heard him howl in her ears. She smelled his blood, rancid sweat, and scorched flesh an instant before his chest heaved a last terrible time and then collapsed with his last fetid breath.

Sue rolled the great mound of flesh away from her with loathing and disgust. She tried to stand, and fell back to her knees, pistol dropping into the tall grass. Then she lay down and turned her face to the sky and tried not to weep with gratitude. The two horsemen were dead and she was alive. Somehow, she was alive!

Perhaps a minute, perhaps even ten minutes passed as she lay with her face upturned and her cheeks wet with tears. Then, Sierra Sue got a firm grip on her mind and struggled drunkenly to her feet. She staggered to the crest of the ridge, where she collapsed. Her dark eyes studied the soddie, where she knew her brother was either dead or very close to being dead, and gradually her heart slowed to a strong and steady beat.

"How many of you are left down there with Bob?" she asked out loud.

Only the crickets in the grass answered, and she knew that there was just one way for her to find out if her brother was alive or dead.

Sierra Sue stood in full view of the soddie, knowing and not caring that she was silhouetted against the skyline. Then, taking a deep breath, she turned back to the single horse that stood some fifty feet away. It looked as scared and bewildered as she knew she must also appear. The horse had carried the smaller horseman to his death, and now she needed to catch that animal and find out if it would also carry her to her own death.

But at least she now had a rifle. The giant's horse, which Sue had been forced to shoot in the heart, was still floundering in its last death throes, and Sue reloaded her pistol and mercifully put the animal out of its misery. There was no point in trying to be silent anymore, not after what she had just done to two dead bounty hunters.

A few minutes later, Sue had both of the bounty hunters' rifles, and the giant's pistol tucked securely under her belt. Sunset was stealing across the prairie, and when the light from the west turned hard on her back, she would gallop down to the soddie praying she would find her brother still alive. And maybe if the sun was straight into her enemy's eyes, and her luck held for one more hour of this day, she would confront more bounty hunters and kill every last one of the bloody sonofabitches.

Chapter 10

When Cutter heard the gunshots and saw Mace and Jake Poole both go flying off their running horses, his first thought was that now he would not need to kill his companions so that he could have *all* the holdup money.

But then, a few minutes later, he saw the woman mounted on Jake's roan come galloping down the hill toward the soddie with a rifle in her fists. Cutter was no coward, and he was pretty damned good with a pistol or a rifle, but he immediately realized his own dilemma. If he did manage to kill the woman, he'd lose sixty thousand dollars worth of stolen bank money. The alternative was that she would kill him just like she'd somehow managed to take down Mace and Jake Poole. To Cutter's way of thinking, the second alternative was far worse than the first.

So he held his fire and let the woman gallop down to the soddie and burst inside. Of course, she would find it ransacked and her brother missing. That was when Cutter thought maybe he could make his play. Jake Poole's roan trotted over to the corral to join the palomino mare.

Just as Cutter had predicted, the beautiful woman burst back out of the soddie with the rifle in her clenched fists. "Bob!"

"I got him!" Cutter shouted from his hiding place in the stand of cottonwoods. "I got him right up here and I'm gonna kill him unless you throw down that rifle and come up here with your hands in the air."

Sue retreated into the soddie and leaned against the cool dirt wall. First and foremost, she knew that she was safe here. The place couldn't be burned and the walls were two feet thick, so that no bullet was going to penetrate them. There was even a water barrel that she knew was half filled, and food in the crude cupboards.

Yeah, I can hole up here longer than he can, but what about my brother? Sue asked herself over and over.

"I'm gonna kill him if you don't come out of there!" Cutter shouted.

Sierra Sue understood one thing, which was that the man up in the cottonwoods would kill her for sure if she gave in to his demands. He wanted the money and, if she told him where it was hidden, there was no earthly reason for him to keep her alive. And if he still needed to know where they'd buried their stolen cash, that also told her that Bob had refused to reveal their hiding place.

"Who are you!" she shouted, angling for time to think.

"That don't matter none," came the reply. "Just surrender or your brother gets a bullet in the brain."

"If I surrender, you're sure to kill us both."

"No, I won't!" Cutter yelled. "I don't give a damn

about either of you. What I want is that sixty thousand dollars you stole from the Bank of Denver."

"What sixty thousand?" Sue was genuinely surprised. "Mister, we took a lot less cash than that!"

Cutter scowled. "Well, that ain't what the bank manager says."

"Then he's a liar."

There was a long pause and then Cutter yelled, "Exactly how much cash do you say you took?"

"Forty-eight thousand."

"That'll do, woman."

Sierra Sue was thinking hard about how she could kill this man and rescue her brother without giving away the bank money. But damned if she could think of a solution. Maybe, she thought, she could strike a bargain with the man hidden in the cottonwoods. A bargain that would save her and her brother and still give them a lot of cash.

"I'll give you five thousand!" Sue yelled. "And you leave us alone."

"Ha!" Cutter said coldly. "I could kill your brother and get that much in a reward! I want *all* the damned money and I want it right now."

"Well," Sue told him, "you aren't getting it, mister. How do those eggs fry up for you? I killed your friends and I'll kill you, too, before the night is over. So what's your call?"

Cutter couldn't believe the woman was winning this argument. He played what he thought was his hole card. "I'm gonna shoot the kid at the count of three if you don't go get me that money. One. Two. Two and a half . . . dammit! Don't you give a shit about your own brother?"

"We never got along," she yelled, almost smiling. "I was gonna kill Bob and take all the money."

Cutter shook his head in bewilderment. "You say you was gonna kill your own brother?"

"That's right."

"Shit," Cutter swore, figuring that he was fast losing the upper hand. "How about we split the bank money fifty-fifty?"

"How about you go straight to hell!"

Cutter was so furious that he unleashed five wild shots down at the soddie, then fired another one into the ground just for good measure. "I just killed your damned brother!" he yelled, seeing no reason not to run another bluff.

"Then I'm coming to kill *you*!" she shouted.

Before he could reload, Sierra Sue was charging out of the front door of the soddie and dashing across the yard with a Winchester in her hands. She disappeared behind the barn. Cutter reloaded his pistol and tried to dampen down his rising panic. The same woman who had just killed his two friends was now coming after him!

"Hey!" he shouted. "Let's make a deal!"

Sue caught her breath. "If you killed Bob, all deals are off, mister!"

"Aw, I didn't *really* kill him. And I've decided that I'll take your five thousand dollars and just ride away."

"How do I know you're not lying again?"

"Well, you lied, too, when you said you didn't care if I killed your brother or not. And five thousand ain't much considering what you took from the bank. Come on, lady, be *reasonable*!"

"All right," Sue decided out loud. "I'll go dig up five thousand and have it ready for you at daybreak."

"It's a deal," Cutter said, only half believing the woman. "And I'll keep my gun on your brother's head in case you try to come up here in the dark and shoot me."

Sierra Sue figured that, if she could get Bob back for five thousand dollars, then it was the safe and smart thing to do. Not that she trusted the man in the cotton-woods to keep up his part of the deal even a little bit. But right now, because she was exhausted and tired of killing, she was hoping that the man who held her brother's life in his hands was willing to carry out his part of this devil's deal.

Sue went back into the soddie, rolled the water barrel in front of the door so that it couldn't be breached in the night, and then she collapsed on the bed that she'd been sleeping on for weeks. She fell asleep almost instantly, and she didn't wake up until the sun was high and she heard the man in the cottonwoods raising all kinds of cussing hell.

Sue moved the water barrel away from the door. She was famished, but clear-headed from her night of deep sleep, and she was willing to bet that the man who held Bob captive hadn't slept even a wink. That, she was sure, gave her a considerable advantage.

"Woman, where's my five thousand dollars, gaw-dammit!"

"I'm going to go dig it up right now," Sue yelled

back. "Don't try and shoot me or you'll never get any of it."

"I ain't that damned dumb!" Cutter screamed, rubbing his burning and red eyes. "Just dig me up the five thousand and get back here pronto!"

Sue checked her weapons. The horse that she'd captured was still saddled and bridled and it was standing near the corral by her palomino mare. "All right, I'm going to get on that saddled horse and go dig it up!"

"About gawdamn time!"

Sierra Sue could hear the weariness in the last bounty hunter's voice. She walked outside, knowing that he could not afford to shoot her down. Moments later, she was horseback and riding the roan toward where the bank money was buried.

Less than fifteen minutes later, she quickly dug up the money, took out five thousand, and reburied her stash so that it couldn't be found. Sue mounted the roan and galloped back to the soddie.

"You got it?" Cutter yelled when she rode into the yard and dismounted.

"I do."

Cutter craned his neck expectantly. "Hold that five thousand dollars up in the sky for me to see."

Sue raised a thick handful of bills. "It's all here, mister. Come on out and get it."

Cutter was tired, but not stupid tired. "Hell, no! You drop the money on the ground and ride back up yonder where the coyotes are probably chewing on my friends."

Sue considered all the consequences of his demand. "How do I know my brother is still alive?"

Bob had come awake in the night, and although his face was badly swollen from his beatings, he was still hog-tied and fighting mad. Cutter had the kid gagged, and now he pulled out the gag and hissed, "Shout out something to your sister."

"Kill him!" Bob yelled out from the trees.

Cutter punched Bob in the ear and yelled, "You hear that? Your brother is still alive."

"I heard him." Sue threw the five thousand dollars down and it scattered across the dirt. "I'm riding away. If you kill Bob, I'll hunt you down and kill you slow, mister."

Cutter believed her. "I'll just take that money and go far away. Your brother is tied up here and you can get him untied when I'm long gone."

"All right," Sue said, noting how vultures were already circling the ridge.

Cutter waited until the woman was almost to the top of the ridge. His eyes kept darting back and forth between her and all the loose money thrown in the dirt. A breeze was scattering all five thousand dollars across the farmyard. Cutter was so impatient to stop the money from flying around that he fairly danced in the cotton-woods.

"All right," he muttered, giving the hog-tied Bob a vicious farewell kick in the ribs with the sharp toe of his boot. "So long, kid!"

Cutter rushed out of the cottonwood trees and went scrambling across the yard, snatching up the money like a kid chasing autumn's falling leaves. He was almost delirious with happiness. Five thousand dollars was a fortune, and maybe he would even double-cross the woman and her brother and get all the bank money! Yes, by jiminy! Why the hell not!

Cutter was so caught up in running after the money that he completely forgot about the woman on the ridge. He didn't see Sierra Sue when she reversed direction and started trotting toward the hardscrabble Wyoming homestead. Didn't see her when she dismounted and sat down less than a hundred yards from the farmyard, then rested the barrel of her Winchester across her knee, took careful aim, and squeezed the trigger.

Cutter wouldn't ever see or hear another thing in this world an instant later when the bullet tore through his happy, mercenary heart.

Chapter 11

"We can't stay here for even another day," Sierra Sue announced to her brother. "The vultures feeding off that dead horse will attract attention for miles. So we'll bury the bounty hunters. There's nothing we can do about that horse I had to shoot."

"Maybe we should just leave those three dead bastards where they lay. I can guarantee you if they had killed me, they wouldn't have gone to any extra bother. They were hard, evil men."

"I know, but I can't just leave them for the vultures and varmints," Sue replied, looking around. "It wouldn't be the Christian thing to do, and we're better people than those bounty hunters. So we'll bury them in that stand of cottonwoods where they held you hostage, then cover their graves with a foot or two of dead leaves so they can't ever be found."

Bob nodded in reluctant agreement. His face was so swollen and purple from the merciless beatings he'd received at the hands of the bounty hunters that he didn't really give a damn about the three bodies. If it didn't sound so crazy even to himself, Bob would have shot and killed all of them a second time just for the simple satisfaction.

"They must have murdered the sodbuster that we bought this poor homestead from," Sue said. "I found a couple of hundred dollars worth of cash and a new pistol and holster."

"That sodbuster didn't deserve to die. He was a good and humble man that had a lot of hard times," Bob said. "I was sure hoping he would make it to California and the Pacific Ocean."

"Me, too."

"So are we heading out for California?"

Sue toed the dry dirt in the yard. "I want to," she told her kid brother. "Lake Tahoe and the Sierras are calling strong to me. But I'm not sure that would be the smart thing for us to do."

Bob shrugged. "Why not?"

"Because I had a conversation with a big United States marshal a few minutes before we did that bank robbery."

"The one whose head you cracked with the barrel of your gun?"

"Yeah. And I told him that I was from Lake Tahoe."

Bob's jaw dropped in amazement. "You what!"

"Stupid. Stupid. I know. But my mind was on the robbery we were about to pull off and it was distracted. And he was such a handsome fella with such a nice Southern way about him that ... well, I just wasn't thinking straight."

"Why didn't you tell me about this before?" Bob demanded.

"Because you were under enough strain as it was," Sue replied. "And I thought I needed some time to sort out what our next move should be."

"Well, dammit!" Bob swore. "If you told a lawman about Lake Tahoe, I sure as shootin' don't think we'd better go back there. That's the first place they'll be lookin' for us."

"Probably."

"There's no 'probably' about it, Sue! And if we can't go back to Lake Tahoe, then where *are* we going?"

"I have no earthly idea." She walked over to the corral. "What I *do* know is that we just can't go back and I can't keep my palomino mare. There aren't that many of 'em in this hard country and she's a golden flag. A sure tip-off of who we are and what we've done. Every bounty hunter is looking for a horse like my mare. And it's too risky to ride into Laramie and try to sell her. Besides, for once, a lack of money isn't our problem."

"You're right about that. But I know how much you love that horse. Are you just going to leave her out here on the prairie?"

Sierra Sue turned to her kid brother, bitterness edging into her voice. "Do you have a better idea, Bob?"

"No."

"Me neither." Sue walked over to the corral gate and swung it open. She marched inside and began waving her arms and shouting. "Come on out of there and run free!"

The palomino bolted past Sue and took off running.

"You think she'll be all right?" Bob asked as the mare galloped across the yard and into the tall grass.

"If it was winter, then I'd say no. But it's still early in

the summer, so I'm sure that mare will do just fine. Some lucky fella will catch her in time, and when he puts a saddle on that mare and actually rides her, he'll think he struck pure gold."

"Yeah," Bob said as they both watched the mare disappear, "they surely will."

"Now that's done," Sue told her brother, "I think we ought to pack up our things and get on the prod. Your horse is of a common color and I'll ride the horse of the man I killed out there. That other horse, which probably belonged to the sodbuster, isn't worth bothering about."

So they buried the dead under the cottonwoods, packed up their supplies and all their ammunition, and rode away from the soddie. At the crest of a hill, Sierra Sue reined in her horse and looked back at the sad little homestead.

"What are you thinkin', sis?"

"I'm thinking about all the heartache that little abandoned homestead has seen," she answered. "Mr. Gray, the sodbuster, said he lost his wife there, and now we planted three more in unmarked graves. It's a pretty homestead. I believe I could have stayed there."

"That's silliness talking," Bob said. "You'd go crazy out here on the Wyoming prairie. You love the pines . . . we both do. We're *mountain* people, only now we can't go back to our mountains."

"Well, we are in the Rocky Mountains. I say that we skirt Laramie and then ride south into the heart of the Rockies."

"Closer to Denver?"

"Not close. I've been told the Rockies run a long, long way to the south. Nearly to Mexico."

"But we'd be heading south in the direction of Denver. You think that's such a smart thing to do?" Bob asked.

"I don't know what's smart or dumb right now. Killing those three bounty hunters has laid a deep sadness on me. So deep that I might never be able to shake it."

"You did what you had to do. If you'd failed, we'd both be dead and those bastards would have left us to rot."

"I know," Sue answered. "But I've learned that killin' humans puts a deep scar on your soul, even when the ones you shoot down needed the killing."

Bob looked over at his sister through eyes that were almost swollen shut, and nodded. "I wish it was me that had shot all three of 'em. They beat me half to death and I'd have laughed when I shot them down."

"No, you wouldn't have," Sue told him. "You're too decent a person for that."

Bob wasn't sure that was true or not, and he didn't see any point in arguing about it, so he said, "Let's go dig up all that bank cash! It'll raise our spirits again."

Sierra Sue managed a smile. "Maybe it will, Bob. Maybe it will."

Chapter 12

"All aboard!" the conductor of the Union Pacific train bound for California shouted at the throng of waiting passengers.

"It's time," Longarm said to a young couple that he had been talking with while waiting to switch trains. A day earlier, he had taken the Denver Pacific Railroad north to Cheyenne, and now he was getting on the Union Pacific, which would take him across Wyoming, then northern Utah, and finally the Great Basin of Nevada, all the way to the Sierra Nevada Mountains.

"My wife and I will join you in the dining car this evening," the man, whose name Longarm had already forgotten, said. "About eight o'clock."

"Sounds good," Longarm told them as he grabbed his travel bag and started for the train. "We'll have a layover in Laramie while they top off the boilers. It's a hard pull across the Laramie Mountains, and then it's almost flat all the way to Reno, Nevada."

Longarm had his ticket punched and found his private compartment. Although he was now a big man in a small space, he lay down and immediately fell into a short and dreamless sleep. When the train pulled into the little timber and ranching town of Laramie, Longarm got off the train and walked into the main business section, where he figured he would buy a good, cheap supper and do some shopping before returning to the train. He had made this journey so many times, he knew the best places to eat and was well known by the business owners. Longarm particularly enjoyed visiting a shop called The Shooter's Den, where an old lawman friend of his sold new and used firearms at very reasonable prices.

So after an excellent bowl of chili washed down by two glasses of beer, he reacquainted himself with the gunsmith, whose name was Fred Holt. Fred was a former U.S. marshal, and he enjoyed catching up on the latest in law enforcement goings-on in the West. For Longarm, it was a must stop, as Fred had his ear to the ground and knew all the latest news related to law enforcement in Wyoming. Longarm was hoping that Fred might have heard something useful concerning the brazen daytime robbery at the Bank of Denver.

"How you doin', Fred!" Longarm called, glad that the gunsmith was busy at his workbench without the distraction of customers. Sometimes, Fred's small gunsmithing shop was so crowded with shooters that it was impossible to talk to the man in private.

Fred was of average size, and his most remarkable feature was his missing left ear, cut off by a desperate escaped fugitive that he'd tracked down and arrested in Santa Fe. Other than the ear, Fred Holt was just an ordinary man who loved, and was widely respected for, his fine gunsmith work.

"Why, if it isn't Marshal Custis Long!" the gunsmith said, breaking into a broad grin. "It's been what . . . four or five months since you've been through Laramie?"

"Closer to six," Longarm said, shaking his old friend's hand.

"Ouch!" Fred cried, pulling back his hand. "My gosh, Custis, you don't have to squeeze a man's hand like you was trying to squeeze a drop of milk from an old dry cow."

"Sorry."

"Don't be," Fred replied, shaking out the pain in his hand. "I've been getting arthritis in both my hands, and some days the pain is worse than others. Today is one of the bad days, and that makes it difficult to work at my repair bench."

"Sorry to hear that, Fred," Longarm said.

"Comes with age. Comes with age and these long Wyoming winters. What brings you through town this time . . . or can I ask?"

"Sure you can ask. It's that big bank robbery we had a while back in Denver."

"Oh, yeah." Fred spent so much time talking to customers about guns that he had a well-used padded stool on his side of the counter and a coffeepot that was always on low boil. He sat down on the stool and leaned on the counter, looking intently at Longarm. "Want strong coffee?"

"No, thanks. I'm catching the train to Reno in a few minutes."

"Reno, huh? Is that where you think the bank robbers went?"

"I don't know. I got hit on the head so hard that I lost

my memory, but it's coming back and I keep remembering something about Lake Tahoe. Might be a fool's journey, but I can't think of anyplace else to start hunting for the bank robbers, and the government is paying for my time and my travel expenses."

"Even if they're not there, I hear that Reno is a fine town to visit. When I was working for the United States government out of your Denver office, they would never come up with enough travel money to get us out of Colorado."

"Given the amount of money taken, this case is a high priority, and so far no one has been able to find the thieves. Besides that, Lake Tahoe is one of my favorite places in the world."

Longarm frowned and then added, "You haven't heard any talk or rumors about the bank robbery, have you? There was a beautiful woman with long black hair and her kid brother that got away with all the money. She was riding a palomino mare and he rode a tall bay gelding."

"Both of 'em young?"

Longarm nodded. "She was said to be in her mid-twenties and her looks were striking. He was in his early twenties and a real handsome fellow."

Fred poked a finger at his old friend. "But not half as handsome as you and me. Right!"

Longarm knew a laugh was expected, and he did not disappoint the gunsmith. "But did you hear of anyone spending a lot of money or fitting that pair's description?"

"Actually, I read a little about the robbery in our

Laramie weekly and knew a few of the details about the holdup and the suspects."

"They aren't 'suspects,'" Longarm told his ex-lawman friend. "Three men and a beautiful young woman walked into the bank. I was standing outside of it and when I went in, the holdup was in progress. I shot and killed two of the robbers, and the woman and what we believe was her kid brother took all the money and escaped."

"Sixty thousand is a huge haul."

"It was actually less than that, but still plenty. So you haven't heard of anyone that fits the descriptions of the woman and her brother?"

"No," Fred answered, rolling a smoke and offering his makings to Longarm, who declined, "but I have heard something that might tie into it."

"Shoot."

"Well, Custis, just a few days ago, there was a simple sodbuster named Homer Gray found shot to death in a shallow grave north of here. And before he was shot, he was spending money every night in a saloon."

"Which one?"

"The Bear Claw."

"I know it well," Longarm replied. "So how does this sodbuster's murder fit. . ."

"Let me finish," Fred told Longarm, holding up a hand for silence. "It seems that this sodbuster, Homer Gray, was a bachelor who had sold his homestead to a pair of strangers for *one thousand dollars*."

"What's so interesting about that?"

"What is interesting," Fred said, "is that homesteads

up in that part of the country where the sodbuster had lived are being abandoned or sold for pennies on the dollar."

Longarm scratched his head. "I still don't see how this sodbuster's murder and the bank robbery might be connected."

"Maybe they aren't," Fred admitted, lighting his smoke. "But here is the rest of the story. When Homer's body was found, three sets of tracks led north, and guess what was found next."

"I have no earthly idea."

"The marshal and his deputy uncovered the graves of three dead men near the soddie. They were well hidden in a cottonwood grove. A saddled horse had been shot out on a ridge and was being eaten by vultures, coyotes, and crows."

Longarm frowned. "What am I missing here?"

"You're missing what I haven't told you, and that is that the three dead men had all taken up with that poor sodbuster at the Bear Claw and they were well known and notorious *bounty hunters*."

"Holy cow!" Longarm breathed. "Do you think that the three bounty hunters found the bank robbers and were killed in a shoot-out?"

"Well," Fred answered, throwing up his hands, "the marshal says that it was either that, or they ran into some other bounty hunters and got into a bad fight."

"That doesn't make a lot of sense unless there was some money in it," Longarm mused aloud.

Fred nodded. "That's exactly what I thought."

"Is your marshal in town right now?"

"Sure is. Name is Bert Tucker. He's a good man. Not

real smart, but he's tough and fair. I like him and when you tell him you're a federal marshal, he'll cooperate and give you the straight story."

"I should go and talk to him right now. Trouble is my train bound for Reno is pulling out in ten minutes."

"Why go all the way to Reno when the bank robbers might still be in Wyoming?" Fred asked.

"Good point." Longarm checked his pocket watch. He sure didn't want to miss his train if this lead was only a dead end. On the other hand, if the deaths of the sodbuster and the three bounty hunters were connected to the bank robbers, then he might have just caught a very lucky and totally unexpected break.

"Yeah," Marshal Tucker said, steepling his fingers and fingering his shiny badge, "I rode up north with my deputy and found all those rotting bodies. Someone else ahead of us found the sodbuster in his shallow grave on the prairie, but me and my deputy, Josh Potter, we're the ones that followed the tracks to the homestead and discovered what was left of the three bounty hunters."

"Tell me *exactly* what you found."

Marshal Tucker described digging up the dead bodies, and ended his account by saying, "Two of 'em were shot with a damned pistol."

"A pistol?" Longarm asked. "That's surprising."

"Sure was," Tucker agreed. "And the dead horse we found was also put down with a pistol to the heart. The third bounty hunter was shot with a rifle. Blew a hole right through his heart and he was probably dead before he hit the ground."

"Did you find tracks leaving the homestead?"

"Sure did. Lots of 'em. But it had rained hard a couple days earlier, and we couldn't tell which might have belonged to the sodbuster or the bounty hunters or whoever the hell killed 'em."

"Did you check out the inside of the abandoned soddie?"

"Of course!" Tucker said, looking a bit offended. "I ain't wet behind the ears. I've been a lawman for longer than you, I reckon."

"No offense meant," Longarm said, not wanting to ruffle the man's feathers and lose his valuable cooperation. "I just had to ask."

"Well, we did do a pretty thorough search of the soddie and surroundings. The soddie had been ransacked and was a mess."

"No papers or anything to give us a clue as to what happened?"

"None. I did some investigating here in Laramie when we returned, and we are sure that the three bounty hunters followed the sodbuster out of town one morning and murdered him on the prairie. Homer Gray was a fool, and he had that sale money he was burning through at the Bear Claw Saloon like there was no tomorrow."

"For him there wasn't," Longarm said.

"Yeah, I reckon that's true enough," Tucker replied. "From what everyone said, he was a good-hearted fella and it's a shame that he was killed all alone out there for his sale money. I don't know how much money he had on him when he died, but it was probably a considerable amount even after he'd bought so many drinks at the Bear Claw."

"What I'm really interested in," Longarm told the lawman, "is who killed the bounty hunters and why."

"That'd be interesting, all right."

"I'm wondering if it was the same two thieves who held up the Bank of Denver."

"I was wondering the same thing, but I heard one was a beautiful woman on a palomino and no one fitting that description was ever seen in my town. And if she was here, I guarantee you that she would be well remembered."

"I expect that is true. Has it been raining any more since you were up at the homesteader's place?"

"Nope. Not a drop and we could use more rain. Might be another drought this year, and that would drive out the last of the sodbusters and poor farmers in this country."

"How far north is the sodbuster's homestead?"

"About a day's ride. I can tell you how to get there, but I promise that you won't find anything new to help you in your investigation."

"I'm sure I won't," Longarm said, "but I have to take a look. It's what I was sent to do, and I don't have a single lead so far in the case."

"Be my guest. I can't ride up with you and neither can my deputy. His wife is about to have their first baby, and I need to stick to my office more or people in Laramie might decide they need a new town marshal."

"I understand."

Longarm received good directions to the sodbuster's homestead, and then said a quick good-bye to the helpful lawman. He hurried over to the train station, cashed

in his ticket to Reno, and waved at the westbound train
as it was pulling out of the station. He hoped the nice
couple whose names he'd forgotten would see him and
realize he would not be joining them for a leisurely evening meal and drink in the dining car.

Then he wired a telegram to his boss, Billy Vail, in
Denver, telling him about the new development in the
case and briefly explaining why he thought he had to
ride up to the dead sodbuster's homestead and take a
look at the scene of the murders for himself.

"If this turns out to be nothing and I've wasted my
time and money on a rented horse, then Billy isn't going
to be too happy with me," Longarm told himself out
loud as he headed for a livery stable and made a note
to also pay a quick visit to the general store and buy
a few supplies. Also, he'd go by his friend Fred Holt's
gun shop and purchase a good used rifle and ammunition. He sure didn't want to be caught out in the open
and shot to death by whoever had killed the bounty
hunters because he had no long rifle.

Chapter 13

Because he'd gotten a late start out of Laramie, it was sundown when Longarm trotted his rented Appaloosa horse over a grassy knoll and saw the vultures squabbling over the remains of a dead horse. Longarm touched his heels to the Appaloosa gelding and galloped hard toward the rotting horse, sending the vultures screaming and wheeling low against the blue sky.

The smell of death and decay was horrific. The Appaloosa was badly spooked by it, and Longarm had to ride the animal a little ways off and tie it to a scrub pine. Ignoring the angry squawks of the vultures, he walked over to the dead horse and studied the ground, trying to read some sense into what might have happened here. The fact that Laramie Marshal Tucker and his deputy had already circled and studied the site made it impossible for Longarm to learn anything, except that the dead horse had been shot through the heart and most likely with a pistol.

Next, Longarm turned and studied the humble little soddie off in the distance. He was almost certain that it would still be abandoned, but he went back to his Appaloosa, pulled his rifle out of its scabbard, and called to the house just to make sure it was unoccupied.

"Silent as a tomb," he said to the gelding. "Ain't nothing left here other than the ghosts of the dead."

Longarm dismounted and loosened his cinch. He glanced at the setting sun, and decided that he wasn't going anywhere else today and that he might as well go inside and see if there was a bed. In the fresh light of early morning, he would make a very thorough inspection, not only of the soddie but also of the yard and surroundings.

It was clear from the chaos and overturned furniture that the soddie had been thoroughly searched and ransacked. Longarm pulled a straw mattress outside because the dark earthy interior of the place made him feel like he was sleeping in a grave. He unsaddled the gelding and turned it loose in the corral, pleased that there was a pile of grass hay left behind. Then he walked over to the stand of cottonwoods and saw the three graves. Marshal Tucker and his deputy had identified the bounty hunters and then had reburied them; Longarm could understand why they had not wanted to haul the rotting corpses back to Laramie.

The homestead was as depressing as a morgue, so Longarm dragged a bunch of branches, limbs, and leaves from the cottonwoods and built himself a huge bonfire right in the farmyard. He had brought cans of peaches and chili, along with some good whiskey.

As the sun went down, it grew cool and the stars came out brightly. The fire roared whenever he threw an armful of leaves on the flames, and up on the ridge where the dead horse lay, the coyotes came from miles around to feast and howl.

At first light, Longarm made a cold breakfast of bread and tinned meat. Then he started his investigation in earnest. He briefly considered digging up the bodies of the three bounty hunters, but his mind recoiled at the idea, and he doubted that they would have given him any fresh or valuable information. Instead, he carefully examined the area, and soon found a length of rope and spent cartridges. From the scattered leaves and splashes of dark, dried blood, it was pretty obvious that a grim struggle had taken place here, and Longarm had a hunch it was between the woman and the bounty hunters or else her brother and those same three men.

Longarm's first instinct was that the bounty hunters had captured the woman while her brother had been off somewhere hunting. But then Longarm remembered the woman and the brother, and something told him that the kid had been the one held hostage and it was the pretty woman who had killed the bounty hunters.

Longarm had bought two pounds of grain, which he fed to the Appaloosa before he saddled and remounted. He rode a huge circle around the homestead and found the tracks that he'd been hoping for, and they led southwest. A mile farther on, he also came upon the palomino mare and another horse, both unsaddled but wearing halters. The pair of horses were grazing in a meadow by a clear stream, and when Longarm rode the Appaloosa toward them, the two animals came galloping up to greet him.

"The woman left you behind," Longarm said, dismounting and catching up the palomino. "Given your good looks, that must have been a hard thing for her to do."

Longarm decided that he would take the palomino with him, if for no other reason than it was always nice to have a relay animal when you were moving fast on a hot trail.

And now he did have a trail. The woman and her brother had made no attempt to cover their tracks, and the tracks, surprisingly, were still heading southwest. Not straight for Laramie, but in that general direction.

"Maybe they're heading down to catch the Union Pacific somewhere west of Laramie. Like Elk Mountain or Rawlins. They could board the train there and be half-way to Reno by now. Hell, they might even have boarded the same train that I was supposed to ride."

The idea that the woman and her brother, with all that bank cash, might be sitting in a dining car enjoying the view and a fine meal, while he was being left behind way out here on the prairie, did not set at all well with Longarm. So he urged his two horses into a steady, ground-eating jog and set off to follow the tracks before another storm washed them away. The third horse tried for a while to keep up with their pace, but quit after about two miles and was soon lost from sight.

As he rode hard toward the distant railroad tracks, Longarm could see dark thunderheads rising up in the sky to the south. He set his Appaloosa gelding into a gallop, and the palomino mare easily stayed beside him, as light and airy as a dancing moonbeam.

The tracks of the two robbers led him twenty-five miles south to a fading railroad town named Diamond. During

the town's heyday years, when hundreds of Irish track-
layers and other workers had been slamming down rails
in a race westward against the Central Pacific and its
Chinese workers, Diamond had been a hell-on-wheels
town. Like most of the towns along the Transcontinental
Railroad route, the town had died as quickly as it had
boomed when the railroad building crews had moved
on. Now, Diamond was little more than a few saloons
and businesses. There wasn't a church nor was there a
school. More than a dozen harsh Wyoming winters had
quickly reduced its few remaining buildings to faded
ruins.

It had been a hard ride down from the sodbuster's
abandoned homestead, with the wind in his face early,
and then driving rain making the ride miserable. When
Longarm rode into Diamond, casting a long shadow, he
was wet and shivering, wanting nothing more than food
and shelter for himself and the two hard-used horses.

He found an abandoned livery, and rode under its
sagging and leaking roof. Finding a couple of dry stalls,
he listened to the rain intensify and heard the boom of
rolling thunder. Longarm put the horses up and fed them
the last of the grain he'd bought in Laramie. He also
found a couple of old feed sacks, which he used to wipe
the two fine animals dry.

"I'll sleep here tonight and see if I can find you a better breakfast tomorrow morning," he told the animals as
he picked up his rifle and headed through the driving
rain toward the closest saloon.

There were five men and a fat whore in the saloon
when Longarm burst through the front door looking half
drowned; all conversation stopped as they studied him

warily. He wasn't wearing his badge, but he was a stranger. It was the whore who made the first move, and she waddled over to force a smile.

"Howdy, big fella! What were you doing out in a storm like this?"

"Oh, just waiting to catch some fish," he said off-handedly.

"Huh?"

"Only kidding. Sorry for the bad joke. Can a man get whiskey and a meal here?"

"He sure can," the whore said, giving him a broken-toothed smile that was supposed to be seductive. "And he can get a taste of *me* if he's got some jingo and love juice in his jeans."

"Well, I've got the jingo," Longarm said, noting that the whore looked old enough to be his mother and smelled old enough to be his grandmother. "But all I want is food and drink and maybe a little friendly conversation."

The whore was persistent. "I'm better in the sack than you might think. I'm a *very* experienced woman, sorta like Cleopatra."

"Cleopatra, huh?"

"That's right."

Longarm had a sudden urge to tell this whore that she looked about as old as Cleopatra would be by now, but that would have been cruel, so he just slipped her a silver dollar and said, "Go find Anthony and make him happy."

Her eyebrows were absent, and she'd painted big arching black lemon slices where they should have been. Now, the slices lifted in a question and her fat hand reached out to cradle his crotch. "Why not you, handsome?"

"Ouch!" he cried, jumping back.

"What's wrong with you, mister?"

"I've been riding hard for two days in mostly bad weather and my privates are rubbed raw and on fire."

"Shoot, big boy, I can cool 'em down real fast."

"Maybe you could," Longarm said, "but I'm gonna soak 'em in whiskey and horse piss as soon as I have a drink and leave."

Her jaw dropped. "You're gonna soak your balls in whiskey and horse piss?"

Longarm nodded. "Yep! That's an old Comanche trick I learned. It works real well. I did it last night, too."

For the first time, the whore backed away with a look of disbelief that turned to revulsion. "Well, I don't want any man screwin' me after he's soaked his pecker in horse piss!"

"Yeah," Longarm said, trying to put on a sad face, "that's what all the women say."

"Stranger, you're a real piece of work!"

"Thank you, ma'am."

Longarm went to the bar, which was a cracked door laid across two whiskey barrels. Longarm had seen such bars before, but most of them had at least removed the doorknobs.

"Whiskey for everyone," he said, laying his money down and watching how the other men crowded to the bar. "A bottle of your best."

"That'd be my Old Sidewinder," the bartender said. "And I'll be takin' a nip, too, if you don't mind."

"I don't mind at all."

"Me, too," said the whore. "Ain't every day you get to drink with a man that soaks his prick in horse piss."

"Amen," one of the drinkers said.

So Longarm and the small group of drinkers quickly killed the bottle, and when they all looked at him like expectant puppy dogs, he bought a second bottle and kept the smiles and conversation flowing. By the third bottle, everyone was talking and laughing, including the bartender, who was filling his own shot glass more liberally than anyone else's.

"So I rode down from the north," Longarm began. "Following the tracks of two riders. One was a pretty woman with long, black hair and the other was her brother."

"Sure! They came in here about four days ago and had a drink and a meal. Prettiest woman I ever laid eyes upon—'cept for you, Louise," the bartender quickly added.

Longarm barked a laugh, but he was the only one that did. He cleared his throat. "I'm looking for them. Did they board the train out of Diamond?"

"Nope," one of the drinkers said. "I watched 'em ride out real early the next morning."

"Which direction?"

"South. They rode south."

Longarm frowned. "I was expecting them to go west and probably on the train."

"They didn't," the man said. "I saw 'em leave with my own eyes."

"Did they say anything when they were here?"

"They drank and had a meal. The kid called the woman Sierra Sue. The woman called the kid Bob."

"Last names?" Longarm asked.

"No last names given," the bartender said. "But I can tell you this. They were in a hurry and they didn't mind paying whatever price was asked."

"What did they buy in Diamond besides meals and drinks?" Longarm wanted to know.

"Ammunition. Supplies. One of their horses had a loose shoe and instead of just asking to have it tightened, they wanted both of their horses shod even though the shoes were hardly used. Like I say, they had money and didn't mind spending it."

"You say they left four days ago?"

"Be five tomorrow morning," the man said. "Two days ago, a pair of bounty hunters came by and they were askin' the same questions you been askin', only they didn't buy us any free whiskey."

Longarm tensed. "Two bounty hunters?"

"That's right. Big, tough fellas."

"And you told 'em the same things that you've just told me?"

"Sure," the bartender said. "They weren't the kind of men you'd lie to and then maybe have 'em come back and get even."

"What color horses were they riding?"

"Blacks. Both horses were black and they were real skinny and run-down animals. Those men and their horses looked as if they'd recently put on a lot of hard miles."

"Did they say where they were going?"

"Nope," the bartender answered. "But they rode out like their asses were afire, and they were headed south just like the woman and her young friend. Say, they didn't strike gold down south of us, did they?"

"No," Longarm replied, his mind racing as he considered this new information. So some more bounty hunters had gotten lucky and were now hot on the bank robbers' trail? That was an unwelcome complication, but it was one that neither surprised nor discouraged Longarm.

Five days was a considerable head start, but not an impossible one to overcome. He just wished that he could figure out why the pair of robbers had passed on the chance to get on the Union Pacific and put a lot of fast miles between themselves and any pursuers. And why on earth would they be moving back into Colorado and closer to Denver?

"I need a twenty-pound sack of grain for my horses and a meal tonight that won't send me to the shitter all tomorrow morning."

"I got boiled bean, bacon, and potato stew on the stove," the bartender said. "Only twenty . . . I mean fifty cents a bowl, and it comes with sourdough bread and coffee."

"I'll take a bowl with the bread and a beer."

"Where you sleepin' tonight?" the bartender asked. "'Cause I got a room for only another fifty cents."

"I'll sleep with my horses in the stable."

"Stable is fallin' down and its roof leaks," a man told him.

"Not everywhere it doesn't," Longarm replied, going over to a table and sitting down heavily.

"Say, mister, that last bottle you bought is about all gone," the bartender called. "You good for another?"

"Nope. Just the stew, bread, and beer."

Longarm heard a collective groan from the other saloon patrons. But he didn't care. He wanted to eat and go to sleep. In the morning, maybe the skies would be clear and the sun would be shining. He would leave without too large of a hangover, and now he knew for dead certain that he was after the right pair.

But damned if he could figure out which direction they were running.

Chapter 14

Sierra Sue and her kid brother Bob rode steadily south, crossing the beautiful Medicine Bow Mountains into Colorado and hugging the eastern slope of the Continental Divide. It was as scenic a mountain country as Sue had ever seen and the longer they rode, the more she became convinced that she and Bob could find happiness in the magnificent Rocky Mountains. And with still more than $46,000 in their saddlebags, they could buy a huge ranch or a prosperous silver mine or both.

"I'd like to find and buy a really nice hotel and saloon," Bob commented one afternoon as they followed an old road deeper into the mountains.

"What for?" Sue asked. "You never talked about buying something like that."

"I dunno. It just struck me that the snows up in these Rockies must get a whole lot deeper than we're used to around Lake Tahoe, and the winters will be long and lonesome."

"I'm not sure the snows here will be deeper than we're used to up in the Sierras."

"Think about it, Sue. In this country, we'd ranch from late spring until fall, then sell off cattle or drive them down to lower country. In the winter, what are we going to do with ourselves when the snow is ten feet deep and the temperature is around zero?"

"We'd repair saddles and tack. I'd read and sew. And I like to snowshoe when the wind isn't blowing. We'll be fine."

"Well," Bob said, "maybe you would be, but I'd be mighty bored. I'd rather be in our own fine hotel maybe helping out a little and talkin' to folks."

"Talking about what?"

"You know," Bob said. "The weather. Cattle and gold prices." He winked. "The local girls."

"Ha!" Sue made a sour face. "You would just get yourself in trouble sitting around all winter in a nice hotel."

"No, I wouldn't!"

"I think you would," Sue argued. "And anyway, we can't just buy a hotel or ranch outright."

"Why not? We have more than enough money."

"Because it would raise a lot of suspicions and questions," she told him. "And that's about the last thing we need."

"So what do we do? Bury the money and live poor like always?"

"No," Sue said. "I've been giving that very question some serious thought. I think that we ought to buy a small ranch operation. Something that costs less than ten thousand dollars. And we wouldn't pay for it all cash up front. Nope. We'd finance a loan."

"A *bank* loan?"

"Yep. We'd put down five thousand and explain that we got that money from a rich uncle who died back in the East. That sounds reasonable. Then, over a year or two, we'd just pay off that loan and gradually add money from our hidden stash into the bank until we had it all deposited."

"I got a better idea."

Sue waited, sure she would not like her brother's idea even a little bit.

"Here's what we could do," he said, grinning. "We ride down to Old Santa Fe and buy us a big hacienda and cantina and hire us a bunch of pretty Mexican girls and. . ."

"Oh, shut up," Sue said, grinning. "If I gave you all the money in our saddlebags, it would be gone in a year. You'd blow it, Bob. And then we'd have nothing."

"We'd have had a great time. Maybe we could go to Europe and buy us a big old Irish or English castle."

Sue had heard enough nonsense, so she kicked her horse into an easy gallop and rode out ahead of her brother. Sometimes, Bob could talk nonsense for hours, and she sure wasn't in any mood to listen to it today. Besides, there were storm clouds forming on the horizon and the air was starting to get cold.

Later that afternoon, they came upon a young couple who had been traveling on foot with nothing but a small donkey packing their few belongings. The young wife was in real trouble, pregnant and lying beside the road moaning, while her husband was trying to calm her down. The moment that Sierra Sue saw the woman, she understood that she was about to have a baby without the benefit of a doctor, much less a bed.

The man jumped up when he saw Sue and her brother, and ran to meet them. "You got to help us!" he cried. "Olive is in labor and we're still about eight miles from Silver Creek and a bed."

"What the hell are you doing out here with her in that condition?" Sue demanded. "Are you stupid?"

"I lost my job at the gold mine in Perdition. They just shut it down and laid five of us off and then told us to leave their mining camp. The wife and I didn't have any money saved, and I'd heard that they were hiring miners in Silver Creek. Ma'am, I got to get a job to pay a doctor so that my little Olive can have our first baby! We didn't have any choice but to try and get to Silver Creek, and on top of all our miseries, the weather has turned foul."

"How old is Olive?"

"Seventeen. But she's a strong little woman."

"How long has she been pregnant?" Sue demanded, dismounting and handing her reins to her brother.

"She's not due for another two whole weeks! I was hopin' to get work in a mine right away and have my first paycheck by then. I got to have some money for Olive and the baby."

The miner was a tall drink of water, wearing worn-out boots, pants with the knees patched, and a shirt that was way past mending. He was a nice-looking young man, but right now, Sue could see that he was almost paralyzed with fear and worry.

"I'll have a word with her," Sue promised. "She can't have a baby out here on this forest road in this rainy weather. The baby would die and she might catch the pneumonia and die, too."

"I know that!" the man exclaimed. "But Olive just couldn't walk any farther, and Silver Creek is still a long ways up this road."

"We passed a little settlement less than a mile back," Sue said. "Why in blazes didn't you stop there?"

"Because they don't have a doctor in that settlement. There aren't even any women that could be a midwife. And nobody I talked to wanted to help us none, so we kept walking and then Olive just fell to the road."

Sue didn't know much about pregnant women, but she did know about horses and cattle, dogs and cats that were about to birth. She took a deep breath and said, "What's your name?"

"Asa." The man tore off his battered Stetson and nervously rolled the brim in his big hands. "I'm Asa Clayton and that is Olive Clayton and she's a fine and brave girl."

"She's a girl all right," Sue said. "Hardly old enough to be having your baby."

"But she wanted a baby, miss! She wanted one just the same as I did. But I never wanted it to come into the world like this!" Tears sprang into his eyes and he wrung the battered Stetson like a washrag.

"Calm down, Asa. You're not going to help matters if you fall to pieces in front of Olive. Just . . . just go back there with my brother and help hold the horses and your donkey so they don't run off. We don't need any more complications."

"Yes I will!" Asa ran the thirty feet to Bob and the horses, dragging his overloaded donkey along behind.

"You'll take care of her and help deliver our baby, won't you?" he called to Sue.

"I'll do what I can," Sierra Sue promised as she went over to the pale young woman.

Olive Clayton might have been seventeen, but she looked younger. Her eyes were squeezed shut, and there were tears leaking from their corners. She had bitten her lower lip so hard that it was bleeding. Olive was very pale, and although the air was cold and wet, she was sweating and shaking like an aspen leaf in autumn. Sierra Sue's first impression was that the girl was going to die right here on this muddy mountain road.

"Olive?" Sue whispered, kneeling down beside the girl. "Olive, I'm going to try and help you."

At the sound of her voice, Olive's eyes shot open and she grabbed Sue by the arm with a desperate strength. "Oh, please, don't let my baby die!"

"I'll do everything I can," Sue promised. "But we have to get you to someplace warm, clean, and with shelter from this cold rain. We have to go back to that little settlement. How rapid are your contractions coming now?"

"Every few minutes. Miss, I can't move."

"You *have* to move," Sue told her. "If we don't get you off this road and out of the cold and rain, you and your baby are going to die."

The girl swallowed hard. A contraction came that caused her to arch off the ground and moan.

Sierra Sue turned around and yelled at Asa and her brother. "Bring the animals here and let's get Olive up in the saddle! We've got to go back to that settlement!"

The two men hurried over, and Bob was the one who scooped Olive up in his arms and lifted her like a child into his own saddle. Olive sagged forward, grabbing the saddle horn and looking for all the world like she was about to faint.

"Oh, God! Oh, God! I think my poor Olive and our baby are gonna die!"

Sue turned on the miner. "Shut up, Asa!"

Bob swung up behind the pregnant woman, and he couldn't help but grimace from the terrible beating that he'd taken at the sodbuster's homestead. The swelling in his face was almost gone, but it was still purplish from the bruises. He grabbed his reins and said, "I'll hold Mrs. Clayton up. Let's turn around and go!"

Sue thought that was a fine idea. She ran to her horse and mounted, then went trotting after Bob and the pregnant Olive. Behind her, she heard Asa call out as he tried to pull along his little donkey, but Sue wasn't waiting for the miner. There just wasn't that much time to spare.

They'd found a cabin and barn whose owner brought them food and firewood and then demanded one hundred dollars cash. It was far too much money, but Sue shoved a new hundred-dollar bill into his greedy hands and then pushed him out the door. Olive was in hard labor by the time that they got a big fire going and the cabin started to warm.

"Oh, my God! She's going to die, ain't she!" Asa moaned. "She's the color of a fish's belly. My poor Olive, you—"

"Get out of here, Asa! Go take care of our horses. Bob, find water to boil and then go make sure that there isn't a midwife who can help me."

"Yes, ma'am," her brother said, pushing Asa out of the cabin.

Sue removed Olive's wet and dirty dress, then covered her with blankets, telling the poor girl that she was going to be just fine and have a healthy baby.

"Do you really think so?" Olive asked between screams dictated by her increasing labor.

"I know you'll both be fine. We just can't panic. I'm going to help you deliver this baby."

"Have you had one of your own before?" Olive whispered, clutching her hands. "Have you?"

"No," Sue said with honesty. "But I've helped deliver lots of animals and I don't think that it will be all that different."

Olive just stared at her for a moment, and then to her credit, she said, "I believe in you, miss. I know you will help me get through this. I have faith that you're a good woman and you won't leave me if things get real bad."

"Of course I won't," Sierra Sue promised.

"And if I die, you won't leave my baby and my Asa all alone 'cause they'll need your help. Asa is a good man and a hard worker, but he needs a steadying hand all the time."

"You aren't going to die, Olive. I swear that you won't."

"You're a godsend, miss. I prayed and I prayed for help, and you come along on that muddy road and you're the answer to my prayers."

Sierra Sue didn't want to hear that kind of talk. She

was a bank robber and a hunted woman. She wasn't any
saint either. But neither was she weak or afraid of much
of anything and she would, by Gawd, somehow pull this
girl and her baby through and take care of them, until
they were strong enough to take care of themselves, no
matter how long that might take or what the cost.

Olive delivered her baby two hours later with surprising ease. It was a girl, pink and squawking with anger
maybe, because it had felt the trial her parents had en-
dured.

"She's beautiful!" Olive cried. "She looks just like
Asa."

"No, she doesn't," Sue said. "She looks like you.
Have you got a name for her?"

"No, ma'am. We thought it was going to be a boy."
Olive beamed. "That's what Asa wanted and we'd have
named it Asa. But ... but to tell you the truth, I was
hopin' for a girl."

"Maybe you should name her Olive after yourself."

"No. I never liked my name all that much. What's
your name?"

"Sierra Sue. Actually, it's Susan."

"That's a real pretty name! Would you mind if I
named her Susan?"

Sue was deeply touched. "Are you sure you
shouldn't think about it for a few days?"

"Nope," Olive said, pursing her lips together. "Susan
is a beautiful name, and you're a beautiful and kind
woman to have saved us, so Miss Susan Clayton it is
going to be."

"I'm honored."

"And I'm grateful," Olive said. "Now would you go get Asa in here so he can see what we made together?"

"I will."   •

Asa was so overcome with joy that he wept, and when Sierra Sue looked at her brother, she saw an expression on his face that she had never seen before. Sue could only describe it as a look of wonder.

"They're beautiful together," he whispered.

"They are," Sue agreed. "Why don't we go check on the horses?"

"They're fine. The barn doesn't leak and they've got grain."

"Let's check on them anyway," Sierra Sue told her brother as she led him out of the cabin.

Chapter 15

The bounty hunter pointed down the muddy road to a cabin with smoke curling out of its chimney. "Mister, did I hear you say that a pretty, black-haired woman and a young feller took up in that cabin over yonder a few days ago?"

"That's right. With a miner and his pregnant wife. The young wife was in real trouble, and old Jessie Watkin's got a hundred dollars in cash for them usin' his cabin. Jessie had to supply 'em with enough firewood, food, and horse hay to last two weeks. In return, the tall pretty woman gave him a fresh hundred-dollar bill with no more hesitation than you and I would give a starving man a plug nickel! I heard that the baby was born alive and healthy. A little girl they're callin' Susan, but nobody has been allowed to visit 'em."

"What color of a horse was the woman riding?"

"Bay, I think. Yeah, a bay."

The two bounty hunters exchanged glances, and then stepped away to discuss this matter without being heard. The taller one, named Luke, said, "Even if the woman wasn't riding a palomino, it still has to be the one we've been hunting for."

"Sure sounds like it," Harlan said in hushed agreement. "How many good-lookin' women are runnin' around with fresh hundred-dollar bills to give away?"

"When we take her and the brother by surprise, we got to do it just right," Luke said. "We can't shoot 'em all. Not with the miner, his woman, and a baby in that cabin."

"Well, why not?"

"'Cause it would rile folks up so much, they'd track us down and hang us for certain!" Luke said.

"Yeah, I expect you're right," Harlan said, scratching his head. "Then how in blazes are we goin' to do it?"

Luke listened to the rain hammering on the tin roof and considered Harlan's question for a moment. "We buy a buckboard or little wagon and we tie 'em all up and haul the bunch of 'em to some abandoned mine and make 'em disappear forever. If we do it tonight, this rain will wipe out the wagon wheel marks and no one will have any idea what we done for that bank money."

Harlan's eyes lit up at the idea. "By damned, Luke, you always were the smart one!"

"Then let's not say another word about them and buy us a wagon. We'll drive it up in the dark behind the cabin, catch 'em by surprise, and hog-tie the lot of 'em."

"Even the baby?" Harlan asked with skepticism.

"Naw. We'll let the baby stay with its mother to the end. I don't like the idea of killin' a baby, but sometimes a man has to do what he has to do."

Harlan nodded. "It'd be awful to have to hog-tie a baby and then throw it down an abandoned mine shaft."

"It would," Luke agreed. "But let's not forget that we stand to make over sixty thousand dollars if we do this right."

"Sixty thousand dollars." Harlan said. "Why, we'd be as rich as kings and never have to work another day in our lives."

"Yeah," Luke said. "We'd have all the money we'd ever need and so many women chasin' after us that we'd have to beat 'em off with clubs!"

Both men laughed uproariously, and then they set about to carry out their deadly plan.

It was long after midnight and the rain was still falling hard when Luke and Harlan burst into the cabin with shotguns and candles. Sierra Sue almost managed to grab her gun, but Harlan hit her across the head and she was momentarily stunned.

When her head cleared seconds later, she looked up in time to see Asa attacking the two intruders with a savage paternal rage that went beyond anything she had ever witnessed. And despite the fact that Asa managed to get Luke to the floor and half strangle him, Harlan sank a bowie knife in the miner's back up to the hilt and killed him on the spot.

"All right," Luke choked, staggering to his feet with his shotgun waving at them like the finger of death. "Anyone else want to be a hero and die?"

Olive was screaming for her dead husband, and Bob wrapped her in his arms, whispering, "You can't help Asa. You need to help your baby! Olive, get ahold of yourself!"

Olive somehow pulled herself together. Her eyes

burned so intensely at Harlan that the man had to look away for a moment in shame.

"What are you going to do with us?" Sierra Sue demanded.

"We want that bank money and we want it right now."

"And if I told you that we don't have it anymore?"

Luke stepped forward and slapped Sue across the face, knocking her to the floor. "We'll carve you up, woman," he screamed. "We'll carve you, your thievin' brother, and the woman and baby. We will carve every last one of you up before daylight."

Sierra Sue believed them, and she could see that they'd been drinking and were nearly out of control. Besides, the bank holdup money was in the cabin, and it wouldn't take long for these animals to find it.

"It's hidden under my mattress," she said. "All of the bank money is under the mattress."

"Luke, find it," Harlan ordered.

The bank money was in a canvas bag, and when Luke opened the bag and saw all the big denominations of newly printed greenbacks, his eyes grew round with wild excitement. He yanked a few thousand dollars out of the bag and waved it at his friend. "We're rich, Harlan! We're rich!"

"That we are. You people get on the floor," Harlan said to them. "We're going to tie you up and gag you and then we're leaving."

"You won't hurt Olive and her baby?" Bob asked.

"Not if you do exactly what we tell you, kid."

Bob dropped to the floor, and then motioned for Olive and Sue to do the same. Sue didn't want to, but with two half-drunk and murderous bounty hunters glaring at her, and with poor Asa Clayton floating in a fresh pool of his own blood, there didn't really seem to be any choice.

Chapter 16

Longarm fought the summer rains and then cold winds as he moved higher into the Colorado Rockies. He had no trail to follow, but whenever people had seen Sierra Sue, they remembered her because of her striking good looks. Also, Longarm learned that her kid brother's face was battered and purplish, and that also caused people to stare and then remember the unusual couple. It was obvious to Longarm that the three dead bounty hunters must have beaten the kid half to death trying to make him tell them where the bank money was hidden. The kid had been wise enough to realize that once they had the money, his life would end.

So down through the valleys and up over the high grades Longarm rode, sometimes on the Appaloosa and sometimes on Sierra Sue's beautiful palomino mare. He kept swapping horses every twenty miles or so in order to keep them fresh in case he had to use them in a hard chase.

It was a clear and perfect day early in July when he rode into a small and nameless settlement. Longarm wasn't planning on staying more than an hour to eat, change his saddle to the extra horse, and ask if anyone had seen Sierra Sue and her brother.

The saloon was nothing more than a converted shack. After Longarm had explained who he was and shown his identification, the bartender yawned and said, "So you're a deputy United States marshal out of Denver?"

"That's right. And I'm on the trail of two bank robbers." Longarm described Sierra Sue and her kid brother, making mention both of her beauty and the kid's mending face. "I want to know if anyone here has seen them pass through here."

The bartender twisted around and called, "Hey, Jessie. Maybe this big marshal here will buy you a bottle if you tell him everything you know."

Jessie was a little man with a big chip on his shoulder. In his mid-thirties, with thick forearms, a long nose, and shifty, close-set eyes, he reminded Longarm of a human ferret.

"Yeah? What's he want to know?" Jessie called across the room. He was eating a meat pie and drinking beer.

Longarm walked across the dirt floor and stopped by Jessie's table. In a few words, he told the man about the bank robbery and described the woman and her kid brother.

"How much money did they steal?"

"Over forty thousand dollars," Longarm replied.

Jessie almost choked on his food. "Damn! I should have asked for another hundred dollars for the use of my cabin!"

Longarm took a seat at Jessie's table without being invited. "Tell me all about it."

Jessie grinned and leaned back in his chair, folding his arms across his chest and looking very smug. "How much money is it worth to you, Marshal?"

Longarm's hand shot across the scarred table, and he grabbed Jessie by the shirtfront and jerked him out of his chair. He shook the man and shoved him back down in his chair, nearly toppling him over backward.

"I'm not paying you a damn thing! Now you tell me what you know or I'll stomp the crap right out of you in front of everyone in this room."

"But you're a damn marshal!" Jessie cried. "You're supposed to help people, not beat the shit out of us!"

"Well, I don't much cotton to your insolent manner. Now tell me what you know or. . ."

"All right!" All the smugness was gone now as Jessie threw up his hands. "Take it easy, Marshal. I rented my cabin to the woman and her brother. There was another man, a miner, and his pregnant wife, and she had a baby girl, and then they were gone."

"What the hell do you mean they were 'gone'?" Longarm demanded. "I'm not in the mood for a guessing game."

"Marshal, they were just *all gone*. They had horses and a donkey and all of 'em were all gone one morning in a rainstorm. I knocked on the door of my cabin to find out what was happening, and there was the dead miner layin' on my floor in a pool of his blood. It was a stinkin' mess! I buried the miner, and nobody paid me a red cent for my trouble. So I ain't too happy about how it worked out, even if I did get a hundred dollars from the pretty woman."

Longarm leaned back in his chair. "Bartender!" he roared. "Bring us a bottle of whiskey and a couple of glasses!"

"Yes, sir!"

Longarm poured himself and Jessie drinks, and then he tossed his own down neat and leaned forward on the table. "Jessie, how long ago did they leave?"

"Two days ago this morning. There was a bad rainstorm, but I saw wagon tracks leadin' off from my cabin still cut deep in all the mud. And there were two men looked like bounty hunters who bought a wagon here, and I figured they were the ones that killed the miner and took the others away. Now, I understand why they did it."

"For the bank money."

"Yep," Jessie said, tossing down his whiskey and helping himself to another glassful. "Over forty thousand's a lot of money, Marshal."

"Did you follow the wagon tracks?"

"Hell, no! The road was sloppy and I had a dead man in my cabin. I didn't want any part of what had happened."

"And you didn't care."

"No, I didn't, except for the trouble I had with the dead man. This is rocky country, Marshal. You got to work your ass off to dig a proper grave, and nobody here was willin' to help me."

"You're breaking my heart, Jessie."

Longarm glared at the sorry excuse for a man that sat across the table from him. He had another whiskey, and got descriptions of the men that had bought the wagon and a couple of mules. Then he picked up his mostly full bottle of whiskey, shoved the cork down deep, and headed for the door.

"Hey!" Jessie shouted. "Ain't you even gonna leave me that bottle? Gawdammit, Marshal, you owe me at least that much!"

Longarm stopped at the door and his gun flashed in his hand. It wasn't professional and it was totally unnecessary, but Longarm sent a bullet in Jessie's general direction that caused the ferret to dive into the filthy sawdust and scramble for cover. Longarm laughed out loud. "That's your due, you pathetic little bastard."

Ten minutes later, Longarm was back in the saddle and moving two good horses at a fast trot up the road toward Silver Creek. When he arrived at that town, he inquired about a local constable or marshal, and when told there was none, he asked if there was a newspaper office. There was, and Longarm went there and told the editor, "I'm looking for some folks with a baby."

Small-town editors were always looking for news, and they generally heard all the gossip and knew about the goings-on in their communities. But this editor hadn't heard a thing about Sierra Sue, her brother, or a woman and her baby.

"However, Marshal, I did see two strangers ride into Silver Creek this morning. Real tough-looking sorts. I understand they are in the Bull Dog Saloon right now throwing lots of money around."

"What color horses were they riding?"

"Thin black horses."

"They're the ones I'm looking for," Longarm said. "Point me toward the Bull Dog."

"How about telling me what is going on?"

"Maybe later. You got an undertaker in this town?"

"Barber does that," the editor answered.

"Tell him he just might have some fresh business to take care of."

"When?"

"Oh, in about two or three minutes," Longarm said as he barged out the door.

Longarm was hell-bent on going into the saloon and bracing the pair of bounty hunters, certain that they had the Bank of Denver's holdup money and that they'd also killed Sierra Sue, her brother, and the poor woman and her baby girl. Just the thought of killing an innocent young mother and her baby made Longarm's blood boil so hot that he was nearly beside himself with a bloodlust for vengeance. Sure, he'd recover as much of the bank's cash as he could, but dammit, he'd make these two murdering bastards pay in spades!

But then Longarm had a moment of real clarity, and he stopped dead in the middle of the street and reconsidered his mission and motives. If he killed the two bounty hunters, he would never recover the bodies of the dead baby and the women and the brother. And although money had been stolen and the pretty woman had bashed his head in, Longarm still figured that she deserved a proper burial, and he damn sure knew the baby girl deserved that much.

So Longarm took a few deep breaths and decided that he would make a sincere effort to capture the bounty hunters alive and find out what they had done with the bodies.

Yes, he thought, *that's something I just have to do*.

Longarm wasn't wearing his badge. He seldom did when on an assignment. So he covered the holstered Colt revolver that rested on his left hip, butt forward. Then he made himself slouch just a mite, and walked real slow and a bit unsteady as he made his way into the Bull Dog Saloon. The moment he entered the dimly lit cavern, he saw the two bounty hunters at the bar laughing and drinking and having a high old time spending blood money.

Longarm pretended to be a little drunk, and he'd had enough practice so that he was good at the ruse. He hiccupped and walked unsteadily toward the bar yelling, "Whiskey!"

The bartender gave Longarm an unfriendly glance and tried his very best to ignore him.

"Are you deaf!" Longarm shouted. "Get the lead out of your fat ass and bring me a damn bottle!"

"You sound like you've already had a bottle or two," the bartender snapped. "Get the hell out of here, mister."

But Longarm wasn't going anyplace without the bounty hunters. He laughed drunkenly and laid a silver dollar on the bar top. "A dollar for a whiskey and if you don't bring it quick, I'm gonna tear the hell out of this place and then I'm gonna kick your fat ass!"

"Excuse me, boys," the bartender said to the bounty hunters. "I had better pour that big man a drink or there's gonna be trouble. I don't want this place busted up."

The two bounty hunters studied Longarm a moment, and then the taller one yelled, "Hey, gawdammit, you better get a lid on your mouth or I'll come over there and kick *your* ass!"

Perfect, Longarm thought, swaying as if he was about to topple helplessly to the floor and yelling, "Yeah, well, come on over here and try it!"

Luke slammed his drink down and headed toward Longarm with clenched fists. He was expecting to end the fight with one punch, and it never occurred to him that the fight would end with one punch but it wouldn't be his own.

Longarm waited until just the right instant, and then he threw a straight right off the bar top that struck Luke full in the face and knocked him over backward out cold before he hit the sawdust.

Harlan went for his gun, but Longarm was expecting that, so he snatched his bottle of whiskey up with his left hand and hurled it into the bounty hunter's face. Harlan howled, and Longarm took three steps and drove a wicked right uppercut into the man's chin that snapped his head back and knocked him over a table and chairs. Harlan struggled to get up, and Longarm hit him a second time in the stomach. Harlan went down to his knees gagging, and Longarm drove a knee up into his nose, and the bounty hunter went down for the count with blood pouring down his face.

"Jesus Christ!" the bartender shouted in shock and amazement. "Jesus Christ, mister! You . . . you might have just killed them two!"

"Afraid not," Longarm said, showing the bartender

his badge and dropping all pretense of being drunk. "Bartender, you have a back supply room, don't you?"

"Sure, but—"

"I'm gonna borrow it for a few minutes," Longarm informed the bartender as he dragged Luke through the sawdust and out into the supply room. He returned a moment later and did the same with Harlan.

"Marshal," the bartender shouted. "What are you gonna do to those two fellas in there?"

"Maybe kill 'em if they don't talk fast and straight," Longarm said. He glared at the bartender and then at the other customers. "They're probably gonna scream bloody murder, but if anyone comes to their rescue, it'll be the last damn thing that they ever do."

No one said a word. They simply stared at Marshal Custis Long and swallowed, knowing that it would be folly to interfere with whatever was going to happen in the back room of the Bull Dog Saloon.

Chapter 17

Longarm came out of the back room with bloody fists and the two semiconscious bounty hunters bleeding buckets. Nobody said a word, but instead just stared open-jawed at the sight.

"These men are bounty hunters who were spending money stolen from the Bank of Denver. I've arrested them, and they may have murdered some innocent people and a little baby girl named Susan and her young mother, whose name I have just learned is Mrs. Olive Clayton. They say they didn't kill 'em, but I don't believe their story, and I'm going to take them out into the hills and find out the truth."

The bartender picked up a bottle of whiskey and said, "Marshal, did you just say they murdered a mother and her baby girl?"

Longarm nodded, his face dark with fury. "I'm hoping they didn't, but thinkin' they did."

The bartender slammed the bottle down so hard that whiskey gushed up and spilled on his bar top. "Marshal, if they killed a mother and her baby, we'd like to hang 'em high!"

Several of the other patrons of the bar murmured their agreement, and then a little old man, bent over with the rheumatism and arthritis, cried, "Damn right we would, Marshal! We'll stretch their fuckin' necks!"

But Longarm shook his head. "I'm going to take this pair out to where they say they made the victims all go into a mine before they used a stick of dynamite to cover the entrance. I'll need digging help to see if the people inside the mine are still alive. Are any of you men willing to get shovels and help dig and carry away rock in order to try and save that woman and her baby?"

Every man in the Bull Dog Saloon shouted that he was more than ready to help.

"Then I'll give you five minutes before we leave," Longarm announced. "Bring shovels, picks, blankets, and if you got any medicines, bring them, too."

Five minutes later, Longarm was riding the palomino while his Appaloosa was tied to the back of the wagon Luke and Harlan had brought into town. The wagon was pulled by mules, and the mules had to strain because there were so many grim-faced people crammed into the wagon gripping their picks, shovels, and supplies.

The abandoned mine that the two bounty hunters had used to get rid of Sierra Sue, her brother, Olive, and her baby was about three miles east of town and a hard climb up a winding and narrow grade, but they made the trip in record time.

"That's it," Harlan said, pointing to a hillside covered with rocks and shale. "That's where we got rid of 'em."

"Were they all alive when you forced them into that mine?" Longarm demanded.

"They were," Luke said, eyes downcast.

"That's where they covered up the abandoned mine, and we need to clear away the rubble!" Longarm shouted as men piled off the wagon and hurried toward the hillside. "Everyone get busy!"

"What about those two?" the bartender asked Longarm.

"Take my pistol and guard them while I go help with the excavation," Longarm said.

"I'll do 'er."

Longarm and the men of Silver Creek wasted no time attacking the wall of loose rock. They worked feverishly until they had a faint opening, and the first thing that they heard was the cry of a baby girl. Not long afterward, Sierra Sue, Bob, Olive, and the baby were being helped outside the mine shaft while the men of Silver Creek hollered and shouted with joy.

Longarm went up to the woman bank robber. She was covered with dust and one side of her face was swollen and bruised. "Miss, I'm Marshal. . ."

"I know who you are," Sierra Sue told him. "I remember you well from the little talk we had at the Bank of Denver."

"And then you parted my scalp with the barrel of your gun and almost killed me," Longarm told her. "I'm afraid that I'm going to have to put you and your brother under arrest."

"I expected that you would when you caught us," Sierra Sue said. "Did you get the bank's money from those two?"

"I did. It was hidden in a strongbox on the wagon. I didn't count the money, but it looked like a lot of cash."

Sierra Sue nodded. "It's all there except for maybe a couple of thousand and what that pair spent in the last couple of days."

"I'm glad to hear that," Longarm told her. "The more money I recover, the easier it will be on you and your brother when you go to trial."

Sierra Sue reached into her coat pocket and produced a crumpled piece of paper. "Maybe it doesn't make a damn bit of difference, but I've got a letter here signed by Charles Bodney the Second admitting that his father murdered our father for a mining claim. A few days later, he sold the claim for thirty-eight thousand dollars. He left our family destitute and caused the death of our mother from too many years of hard work."

The letter was short. "You say that banker wrote this letter?"

Sue nodded. "Yes, he did."

"And how much money did you rob from the Bank of Denver that day we met?"

"Forty-eight thousand exactly ... minus a hundred dollars I left for those two fellas you shot so that they could be buried proper."

"Bodney swore that you and your brother stole sixty thousand dollars."

"Doesn't surprise me," Sierra Sue replied. "That just proves that the banker's son is as crooked as his late father."

"Given this letter, you and your brother might only have to serve a brief prison sentence."

Sierra Sue shrugged. "I guess that's some consolation. But I was—"

Her words were interrupted by a gunshot. Longarm whirled, his hand going for his sidearm and finding the holster empty. Damn! He'd loaned his gun to the bartender, only now the bounty hunters both had pistols in their hands and one of them was pressed against the bartender's head.

"Marshal, you tell everyone here that they'd better freeze or I'll blow this man's brains out of his head."

Custis cursed to himself. He should have tied up the bounty hunters instead of letting an amateur keep them covered while everyone attacked the hillside in a desperate rescue attempt.

"All right," Longarm said, "what do you want?"

"We're taking the horses and all that bank money!" Luke yelled. "If you try to stop us, we're going to kill the bartender and then we'll kill as many others as we can before we die."

"They're not bluffing," Sue whispered. "They're desperate and merciless and they'll do exactly as they say."

"Marshal, come away from everybody else and get on over here," Harlan shouted. "Step right up and be quick about it."

Longarm had no choice. He walked toward the armed hunters and the wagon. "Maybe we can work something out," he told them.

In reply, Harlan jumped forward and slammed the barrel of his gun against Longarm's temple. Longarm's knees buckled and he went down.

Sierra Sue tore a gun from a man's holster and charged forward, a cry of rage in her voice. She opened fire on the two men, and they turned away from Longarm and returned fire. A bullet struck Sierra Sue in the left arm and knocked her full circle. By then Longarm was reaching for that deadly pocket derringer attached to his watch fob. It had two barrels and he used them both, firing up from the ground. His slugs tore first into Harlan and then into Luke at exactly the same moment that Sierra Sue's bullets punched into the bounty hunters.

As suddenly as the gunfight had begun, it was over and the bounty hunters lay dead beside the wagon.

Longarm was a little woozy from the blow he'd taken, but he still managed to hurry over to Sierra Sue, who held her pistol at her side. "It's not too bad," he said, tearing her shirtsleeve away and studying the wound. "A bullet passed through the flesh and there's a lot of blood leak, but I'll get it stopped."

"Did it shatter my arm bone?" Sierra Sue asked.

"No."

"That's good," the beautiful bank robber said, managing a smile. "I'd hate to lose my arm and not be able to rope a steer or horse ever again."

"You won't lose the arm . . . just a lot of blood."

"I can spare some of that, Marshal."

Longarm quickly bound up the wound, and then he supported the woman and turned to study the crowd and the people that they'd just saved from being buried alive.

"Folks," Longarm said, his eyes mostly on the kid brother and the young woman that stood beside him crying silently with a baby in her arms. "Justice has been well served here today, and you're all heroes for saving the lives of these people that were buried."

The bartender, who seemed to be the spokesman for the bunch, exclaimed, "Marshal, in all my born days, I never saw anything like this. You and that pretty woman sure did some fast and fancy shootin'!"

"We got lucky," Longarm said modestly.

"Not me," Sierra Sue said. "I *always* hit what I aim at."

Longarm had to chuckle at her words. "Sierra Sue, given that you just saved my life and probably a lot of other lives, and given that the bank's money has almost all been recovered, I'm going to ask the judge in Denver for leniency and to put you and your kid brother on parole."

She stood straighter. "Marshal, do you actually think he'd do that for me and Bob?"

"Yes," Longarm answered. "But he'd insist that someone of authority watch over you and your brother to make sure that you didn't violate the parole or leave Denver on the lam."

"And who'd take that kind of responsibility?" the tall, pretty woman asked.

"I would," Longarm told her. "It would be my pleasure."

Sierra Sue smiled, and then she kissed Custis right in front of the whole crowd. That caused everyone to burst out with laughter and applause.

Bob stepped forward. "Marshal, when we were trapped in that mountain and things looked mighty bad, I promised Olive and her baby that I'd take care of them if we somehow survived."

Because he could feel her swaying from the loss of blood and also fatigue, Longarm slipped his arm around

Sierra Sue's narrow waist. "Bob, right now we need to get back to Silver Creek and find a doctor. But when we do get to Denver, I feel confident that a judge will look favorably on your willingness to take responsibility for the welfare of Olive and her baby."

"I mean to do it," Bob promised, bringing the mother and baby under his arm. "And not just for a short while either."

Sierra Sue's eyebrows shot up questioningly, and Bob just grinned at his big sister. Watching them, Long-arm had the feeling that everything was going to turn out just fine and that he was really going to enjoy watching over Sierra Sue.

Watch for

**LONGARM AND THE PLEASANT VALLEY
WAR**

the 372nd novel in the exciting LONGARM
series from Jove

Coming in November!

GIANT-SIZED ADVENTURE FROM AVENGING ANGEL LONGARM.

BY TABOR EVANS

penguin.com/actionwesterns

M456AS0409

DON'T MISS A YEAR OF

Slocum Giant
by
Jake Logan

Slocum Giant 2004:
Slocum in the Secret Service

Slocum Giant 2005:
Slocum and the Larcenous Lady

Slocum Giant 2006:
Slocum and the Hanging Horse

Slocum Giant 2007:
Slocum and the Celestial Bones

Slocum Giant 2008:
Slocum and the Town Killers

Slocum Giant 2009:
Slocum's Great Race

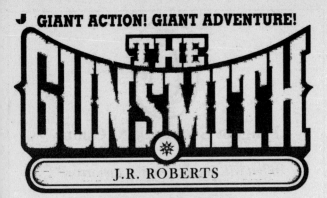

GIANT ACTION! GIANT ADVENTURE!

THE GUNSMITH

J.R. ROBERTS

Little Sureshot And
The Wild West Show
(Gunsmith Giant #9)

Dead Weight
(Gunsmith Giant #10)

Red Mountain
(Gunsmith Giant #11)

The Knights of Misery
(Gunsmith Giant #12)

The Marshal from Paris
(Gunsmith Giant #13)

Lincoln's Revenge
(Gunsmith Giant #14)